I0784177

About the Author

CHRISTIAN J. GONZALES is a poet, filmmaker, novelist, and engineering student who believes in the power of vulnerability as art. A graduate of LAFS, Christian has worked across stage and screen--as a writer, director, and producer--while building an intimate body of literary work exploring identity, trauma, family, and the complex road to self-redemption. His first poetry collection, Smiley--named after the nickname his grandmother gave him--traces the journey from childhood innocence to hard-won self-acceptance. Christian lives in Los Angeles, California, with his dog, Sophia.

66

To Optimus, my late best friend, whose pure heart taught me the strength in being a good human being. Your love shines through these pages

99

TABLE OF CONTENTS

AUTHOR'S NOTE

I *was not supposed to write this book.*

If my past had its way, I would have swallowed every word, buried every memory, and carried on as if nothing had happened. That's what I was taught: to endure, to suppress, and to keep my voice small. To let the world write my story for me.

But I refuse.

This book is my answer to the silence. It is the voice of the child I was, the man I became, and the person I am still learning to be. It is the story of surviving what was never meant to be survived.

I was seven years old when the world stopped making sense. It didn't happen all at once, not in some dramatic, cinematic moment. It was slow and insidious, safety unraveling at the seams and trust cracking like old paint. The people who were supposed to protect me didn't. The hands that should have lifted me up instead pulled me under.

The silence and anger after were the worst parts, stretching for years, taking root in the spaces where my voice should have been.

I carried that silence like a stone in my chest. Like an anchor chained to my ankles. I carried it through childhood, through the slow erosion of my faith, through the quiet collapse of relationships I once believed would last forever. I have lost people, and I have lost pieces of myself. I have grieved things I can never name.

For a long time, when I was younger, I thought pain was permanent. That once something was broken, it stayed that way. That I was a collection of shattered pieces, held together only by habit.

But I was wrong.

We are not just the worst things that have happened to us. We are not doomed to repeat old wounds like a script we have no say in. We are not bound to our suffering like some tragic prophecy.

We can rewrite ourselves.

That is what this book is: an act of defiance, an act of survival. A declaration that I am more than my pain. A soldier with a duty and a purpose.

If you are holding this, if you are reading these words, I want you to know something: You are not alone. You are not beyond repair. And no matter who has tried to silence you, no matter how heavy your past may feel, your story is still yours to write.

- 5 -

POEMS

I Never Wanted to Write This Poem

I never wanted to write this poem.
Did you hear me?
I never wanted to write this poem.
But here I am, standing in front of you,
Because the words—the memories—they burn like fire on my
tongue,
And if I don't spit them out, they'll consume me whole.

Seven.
I was seven years old.
Seven, when the world twisted itself into something
unrecognizable,
When hands that should have lifted me up,
Became chains that dragged me down into the dark.

He was supposed to be family.
You know, family?
The ones who are meant to protect,
The ones who are meant to love you.
But his love was poison.
His love was a fist,
A whispered threat in the middle of the night,
A lie that choked the breath right out of me.
"Don't tell anyone," he said.
Like it was my fault.
Like I was the monster.

I carried that silence like a weight,
And let me tell you—silence is heavy.
It burrows into your bones,
Sinks into your skin,
Until you don't even recognize yourself anymore.

Until you look in the mirror and all you see is the ghost of the
person you could've been,
Should've been.
Would've been.
If only.

But I'm not here to make you pity me.
I'm not here to make you cry.
(Though, if you're crying, I get it—I've cried enough tears to
fill oceans.)
But I'm here because this is the story I never wanted to tell,
The poem I didn't want to write,
And now I'm owning it.

You see, I spent years—YEARS—thinking I was the broken
one.
Thinking I was the one who needed to be fixed,
Like my body was a crime scene
And I was just evidence.
Like my soul was something damaged,
Something irreparable.

But no more.
I said, no more.

Because here's what they don't tell you:
Healing is ugly.
Healing is messy.
It's screaming into pillows and shaking through nightmares,
It's stumbling through therapy sessions and breaking down in
grocery store aisles,
But it's also waking up one day and feeling the sun on your
skin
And realizing—
You are still here.
I am still here.

This body?
This body is MINE.
These scars?
They're mine too.
And I wear them now like armor.
I wear them like proof.
Proof that I survived.
Proof that I can still love, still trust,
Still breathe without feeling like I'm suffocating.

And to every single person in this room who has ever felt the
weight of silence,
Who has ever carried a story they thought would break
them—
I see you.
I hear you.
And you are not alone.

Because we are still here.
We are the fire that keeps burning.
We are the voices that cannot be silenced.

So yeah, I never wanted to write this poem.
But I'm glad I did.
Because I am not the monster.
I am not the victim.
I am the one who got back up.
And this story?
It ends with me standing tall.

Handprints on My Neck

Fear's grip, tight,
like ice, burns white.
I smell the damp earth,
buried 'neath my worth,
torn by roots of doubt.

Voice stripped, night,
falls heavy, no sight.
Air thickens, stale,
a coffin's wail,
whispers cold against my skin.

Speak? No, it's gone,
words choke, wrong.
My tongue, a stone
taste of rust, alone,
can't lift the weight of silence.

Fingers press, cold,
like iron, bold,
they leave bruises blooming,
a scent of blood looming,
copper lingers, sharp and still.

I hear them—cracks,
splintered backs
of thoughts unspoken.
They snap, broken
beneath the strain of restraint.
I fear to tell,
sour on my tongue.
It swells, a shell,
salty sweat runs,
a shiver down my spine.

Held back,
held down, unseen.
My truth, unheard,
each word, blurred,
slipping like sand through hands.

Their grip, strong.
A rancid scent—
nailbeds long, unbent,
scrape down, leaving marks.

I want to scream,
trapped beneath the seam,
the skin between breaths.
Handprints bruise, linger,
tight fingers.

The world spins slow,
the walls close low.
I taste the dust,
a bitter must,
clogging my throat.

I am held still,
still as stone.
The sky above hums,
but no sound comes.

And the ground beneath—
I feel it quake,
waiting for me to break.
And yet—
I feel it, a tremor,
heat crawling,
through my chest,
a whisper,

a breath—still pressed,
but stirring.

The fingers, they tighten,
but somewhere, I see light then,
faint, a thread,
where I am led,
to a place my voice still waits.

The Sepulcher's Embrace

In youth, I bore a chain of blight,
a trinket tight, a tether slight:
Death's own name in silver scored,
a weight, a fate I once adored.

Bound, enwound, in wretched thread,
a whispered vow, a pact unread,
a locket locked, a door unbarred,
a promise frail, yet ever scarred.

Lo! a shadow veiled my sight,
veiled my breath, unveiled the night.
I clutched the cold, I kissed the air,
I danced with dust, slept with despair.

I rang the bell in coffin's keep,
a sound too weak, a cry too deep.
The walls, they pressed, the dark, it laughed,
a hollow tune—a devil's craft.

Tick—tock—tick—
a hollow snare.
A pause, a breath,
no sound was there.

Each sigh, a dirge, a hymn profane,
each breath, a step within the grave.
A curse, a verse, a choking thread,
a lover's name that fled the dead.

Yet in the dark—a hush, a glow,
a bread, a shred of light below.
A flicker slight, a breath, a crack,
a call, a claw that pulled me back.

I gasped, I writhed, I wrenched my hands,
tore loose the chain, the cursed bands.
A strangled spell, a final plea:
"O Death, thou shalt not cradle me!"

The dawn unfurled, the black withdrew,
the winds of fate in silence blew.
And at my feet, in dust confined,
lay ghosts that once had ruled my mind.

Dr. Noose

Oh dear, oh my, just look at you!
So sad, so tired, so bent in two!
Your head's too heavy, your heart's too sore,
Your feet don't like to walk no more!

Well, step right up! The doctor's in!
I've got a trick to fix that grin!
I've got a cure, so fast, so free!
A surefire way to quiet *thee!*

No pills! No shots! No doctor's chair!
No beeping things, no messy hair!
No pokes, no pulls, no yucky goo!
Just one quick knot and—POOF! You're through!

Your worries, woes, all gone—poof, poof!
I'll tie them tight; this is no spoof!
Your thoughts will stop their twisty tricks,
No clocks, no chores, no counting ticks!

I see you frown, oh no, don't pout!
You're in, you're here, no backing out!
I've helped before, I'll help again,
I've helped so many, many friends!

See, Tommy tried and so did Loo,
And Billy? Oh! He did it too!
They came to me, just like you said,
And now they rest their sleepy heads!

But—wait! What's this? What's that I spy?
A beat, a break, a fist, a sigh?
A lake, a cake, a younger you?
You shake, you ache—oh, what to do?!

Aha! Oh ho! A twist, a trick!
A thought just *sparked!* It sparked so quick!
You say you're tired? You say you're through?
But…what if life has more for you?

A book with chapters left to write?
A day with friends, that's oh so bright?
A joke, a hug, a sunny day,
A friend who *wants* for you to stay?!

Oh dear, oh my! This simply *won't* do!
Doctor Noose can't work on you!
You broke the pattern, left the trek,
You climbed back up—you're not done yet!

Oh, silly me! I must have blundered!
I spoke too soon! A life I plundered—
Too much, too fast, too dark, too deep,
For you are meant to live, not sleep!

So, step right down, and take a rest,
Life may be bad, but you are best!
Your heart still beats, your breath still stays,
And you deserve to see more days.

For *you* are light, and *you* are bright,
And *your* bright smile's worth the sight.
Not tucked away, not hung, not tied.
But standing strong. Still here. Alive.

Panic Attack

I can't feel my hands—
Are they still there?
It's too much.
The air—where's the air?
My heart—
No, no, no, it's stopping, I swear.

Look at me.
No, here. Focus on this.
Your hands are there, see?
You're just lost in the mist—
But I'm right here, stay with me.

I can't, I can't—
Something's wrong inside.
What's my name? Why can't I—
Where am I?
What's happening to me?

You're safe. You're here.
Breathe with me, okay?
Feel the ground beneath you, clear
your head. Stay.
Your name is... wait, say it with me.

I don't— I don't remember.
I swear it's slipping—
Everything's gone.
I'm cold, I'm frozen.
Why can't I hold on?

Alright, let's ground you.

Look around.
Name five things,
tell me what you've found.

The clock— it's red.
The chair's black.
The door, it's brown,
with gold around the knob.
And the lamp—white.

Good. That's good.
What else is there?

The rug.
It's green, like grass.

Perfect.
You're coming back
Stay with me. You're okay.

But I feel... I feel faint.
It's still blurry,
But—
I can breathe again.
Barely, but I can.

That's it, just keep going.
The worst is slipping past.
Your breath is yours again,
And you're not lost, I promise.

I'm still scared.
But... less now.
Still shaking,

But I hear you.

Good.
You're okay.
I'm still here, and so are you.
We'll make it through.
Just breathe. Just breathe.

Monster

I huff, my breath an acidic touch,
not to burn, not to harm, but still, it does.
Stand in front of me, and I will warn you,
not because I want to strike,
but because I have before.
And that is enough.

I growl at the sight of your smile,
not because I hate it,
but because some part of me fears it.
I watch joy from the outside,
and in my bitterness, I have ruined it.
I loathe myself for it.
Even as I write, the ink turns to regret.

No, no—
I am not the monster you think I am.
I huff, I growl, I loathe,
but I do not take pleasure in this.
I do not take pleasure in hurting you.
And yet, I have.
And yet, I do.

I feel guilt. I feel remorse.
But these claws, this fire inside me—
I did not ask for them.
I did not want to be this way.
A force beyond me, or maybe within me,
has shaped these hands into weapons,
even when all I wanted was to hold, to heal.

My breath is hot, scalding,
but my touch is soft, like a teddy bear.
But my claws are sharp like a bear.

I have torn where I meant to mend.
I have wounded where I meant to protect.
I have made you fear me,
when all I ever wanted was to be loved.

I am not a monster.
I am not a monster.
I am not a monster.

My Skeleton

My ribs pierce through my flesh
A layer of fat and visceral abscess
that doesn't seem to disappear

The Unnamed Shore

They say no man remembers arriving at the Unnamed Shore.

The sand is black as charred bone, the water thick as ink,
where currents sink and silence drinks the names of men
before.
The sky, if you dare to look,
holds no sun, no moon, no mercy.
Yet the air hums, drums in my chest,
whispers that do not rest, voices that do not rise from the sea.
And the tide moves, bruised and slow, pulling forward, letting
go.

I woke there, though I do not recall sleeping.

The last thing I remember—
No. That is the trick of this place.
It takes, not all at once, but in layers,
in whispers, in wind-stripped prayers,
memory peeling, sealing, revealing what was mine before it
wasn't.
Ghosts slip between the cracks,
shadows stretch, a blade, an axe,
until all that remains is the shape of what once was.

I am not alone.

A woman stands at the water's edge,
her hair tangled in seafoam, arms still as stone,
her fingers clasped behind her back.
She is unmoving, yet the tide curls toward her,
bends, breaks, aches like a thing unloved.
She does not turn when I speak.

"Where am I?"

Her voice is wind through hollow bones.
"You are between."

"Between what?"

Finally, she turns, slow as the tide,
eyes like distant storms, lips that once formed warmth
but now hold ice, twice bitten, twice burned.

"Between what was and what will be."

A riddle, then. I have no patience for riddles,
not here, not now, not with the tide licking at my heels,
with the sand shifting beneath me, restless, breathless,
with the weight of a name I have somehow misplaced.

"Who are you?" I demand.

She does not blink.
"I have been called many names."

The sea groans, a chorus of bones,
rising higher, creeping close.
Something moves beneath the surface, vast, coiling,
a thing without a shape, without a face,
without a past, and I take a step back.

She does not move.

"Tell me your name." I pressure.

"I was once called Thetis," she says, tilting her head,
"And you were once called great."

The name strikes like the clash of steel.

Thetis. Mother of Achilles.
The sea-nymph who dipped her son into the Styx
and made him nearly invincible—nearly, barely,
barely breathing.

"I am not—"

"No," she agrees, before I can finish.
"Not anymore."

A pause. A flicker of something—
recognition, or perhaps regret?
The wind does not allow me to name it.

"Then who am I?"

Thetis watches me, unreadable.
Her hands, pale against the dark waves, tighten into fists.

"That is the question, isn't it?"

The sky splits above us, a crack of light against the dark,
a wound in the heavens, a mouth without sound,
and I suddenly understand.

I am not the first to stand upon this shore.
I am not the first to ask these questions.

The tide does not answer.
The sand does not care.

And Thetis—
Thetis only watches as the sea begins to rise.

Musing

Oh, forlorn! my community be.
So ahead of myself I be,
but behind I feel in life,
Presently laid in the ground.

I scorn the smile on your face,
and covet your youth.
Your ability to pursue it is beyond me.

Pathetic in words,
the anger in misology.
The drowning of death
Is ironically my model of monotony.

Over my shoulder, I sense a dread
born of disappointment
I dreadfully lugged;
like a woeful widow over my shoulder.

She lost her husband,
a self-wallowing
man reluctant to trusting.
A beggarly bee buzzing.

I stretch my wings,
bound by unseen chains;
never to soar as dreams turn dust,
a bitter clown dancing with lust.

A Dying Star

The light slowly flickers in the sky.
There's a metallic smell with almond cookies.
A sense of heavy wind blowing against my skin,
As I take in the death of something
- *billions*- of years old.

It has me thinking of someone I once knew.
If I ever knew them, that is.
Like this light,
they lived a long life.

But light can only travel so fast-
and when you're so far, so distant,
you won't see the death until it's too late.

I think this person's light died,
And I was too far to see it.
At least, until it was too late.

I look at this star and I think of this person.
I still see a flicker of light.
So maybe it's not the end.

I hope it isn't.

For My Father

you stood—
not as a man,
but a monument,
carved from silence.

your love was a closed fist,
a door half-shut,
a winter that never ended.

i learned your language young:
the sigh between words,
the weight of an absent touch,
the way walls can speak louder than men.

you blamed her—
(of course you did)
as if love unravels on its own,
as if the fault is not the hands that pull.

and i was there, a ghost in your house,
watching the collapse.
counting the cracks.
waiting for a voice that never came.

then, the knife of your words—
i will take your name away.
a slash across the skin of who i was.
unmaking.
unbecoming.
undoing me.

but listen,
(no, really, listen)

i do not hate you.
(what a waste that would be.)

i have lived long enough to see
that men like you
are forged, not born—
bent under the weight of their fathers,
folding into steel.

familial love is not always a gentle thing.
sometimes, it is a scar.
sometimes, it is the echo of a slammed door.

and yet,
(and yet)

here i stand, whole despite it all.

so if the years should let our roads collide,
if time grants us the mercy of an unspoken truce,
if you reach, finally—

i will not turn away.
i will be waiting.

but this time,
with open hands.

To My Siblings

We grew up together, yet in different ways,
sharing space, sharing time,
but seeing the world through different eyes.
Love was not always spoken,
but it was there, woven in laughter,
in silence, in the spaces between words.
These are the messages I never said aloud,
the truths that lingered unspoken.
But now, I say them here, for you.

To my stepsister—
I wish I had known you better,
that I had bridged the space between us,
but I was young, and you were older,
and that difference felt like a mountain.
I let the idea of favorites build walls,
never realizing you were just a kid, too,
trying to find your way.
You were there, a quiet presence,
a part of the story even if our pages never intertwined.
I hope you know—
you were loved.
You are loved.

To my sister—
our love was a battlefield,
a war fought in words and teasing glances,
a game of laughter and frustration,
as sharp as it was soft.
But love, real love, never falters,
and through every jest, every push,
every roll of the eyes,
there was always a thread that held us close.
I was told before the teasing, before the battles,

when I was just a baby, too small to understand;
You sang a lullaby, soft and slow,
and held my hand until I fell asleep.
Even then, before words meant anything,
I silenced, I knew I was safe with you.
And no matter where life takes us,
that thread remains, unbroken.

To my brother—
my first best friend,
my rival in play,
my ally in adventure.
Do you remember the woods?
The scent of pine, the call of crows,
our wooden swords clashing
in front of the Grandfather Tree?
The world was ours then—
full of quests and kingdoms unseen.
Even now, when I close my eyes,
I can still hear the rustling leaves,
feel the thrill of the fight,
and see you beside me, fearless.
We have walked different paths,
but no distance, no time,
can unwrite what we were.

To my siblings—
we are stitched from the same history,
woven into each other's stories,
whether through laughter or silence.
I carry you all with me, always.
In memory, in love, in all that we were,
and all that we will be.

The Bridge of Her Dreams

In the quiet shadow of the twilight's sigh,
A bridge, broken beneath the blackened sky,
Crafted from dreams that once soared high,
Now tangled in nightmares, now severed by lies.

A mother and her son, hand in hand,
Stood upon this fragile span,
Built with hopes and a trembling plan,
Woven from threads of a wounded land.

This bridge, her dreams, it used to glow,
Tapestry of hopes, woven slow,
Now fractured, marred by fear's undertow,
Her past's dark secrets in the waters below.

"In this place," the mother whispered, lost,
"I see every hope, every cost,
Every battle fought, every line crossed,
Every dream stolen; every freedom lost."

The son, his face a portrait of resolve,
Knew this bridge could be rebuilt.
If only his mother's past would dissolve,
Into strength, into hope, where their hearts willed.

"Mother," he begged, "let us use the pieces,
Of every hurt, every fear that creases
Your brow, let's mend with what peace is,
And rebuild with the love that never ceases."

But she shook her head, tears cascading down,
"I cannot, my child, my pain is profound,
My wounds are too deep, my chains are unbound,
These ghosts will drown us before we turn around."

"Please, Mother," he cried, "we must be brave,
To rebuild, to cross, we must pave
Our way with all that you forgave,
And with every tear you held back like a wave."

The bridge beneath them trembled and swayed,
The pieces falling where they lay,
In the chasm where her demons played,
A void that stretched both night and day.

And as the shadows reached to claim,
The broken planks that bore their name,
The son took his mother's hand again,
And held it tight through the storm and rain.

"Look at me," he said, his voice a song,
"We are strong enough to right this wrong,
To take your pain, to make us strong,
To build anew where we belong."

But the bridge began to splinter and crack,
The past pulled hard, and the future went black,
She lost her footing, and started to fall back,
Her fear pulling her into the abyss's track.

"No!" he shouted, his grip like steel,
As she slipped from the bridge, from the real,
Her fear, her past, her cries, he could feel,
But he held her tight with all his will.

And in that moment, time froze in place,
Mother and son in a fateful embrace,
Holding on tight in the empty space,
Between the broken and the uncharted grace.

"Do not let go," he whispered low,

"I need you more than you know,
Together, we'll take it slow,
Piece by piece, row by row."

She looked into his eyes, so brave, so wise,
And in them, saw a future, a sunrise,
Where their past would not be a disguise,
But the foundation for their new skies.

"I will try," she breathed, her voice a spark,
As the chasm below them turned from dark,
To a field of stars, a celestial arc,
A new beginning where dreams embark.

And so, the bridge, though broken, remained,
A testament to all they'd gained,
Built with love, despite the pain,
A path forward, despite the strain.

Hand in hand, they stood once more,
Looking ahead to the distant more,
With faith that what they're building for,
Will lead them to a place they've never been before.

A Boy No Older Than Eight

I dreamt a dream last night.
Not one of malice intent,
but one awe-inspiring minute
I will never forget.

The trees stood still except for the soft breeze,
sunlight blotching rays in between leaves.
The air smelt of oatmeal cookies, freshly baked,
While I sat with a young boy, no older than eight.

He looked at the ground, ignoring my eyes.
Passion that was too soon forced to sedate,
I knew his innocence had too soon died.
He was just a young boy, no older than eight.

His eyes were full of sorrow and confusion,
like he felt like life was just an illusion.
One he rejected with fearful haste,
and yet the boy was no older than eight.

I wanted to show him that life was precious,
despite the hateful odes many sing,
So, I reached out, offering a gentle embrace,
Hoping to guide him to a safer place.

His small hand trembled as it met mine,
A bridge formed in that fragile line.
We walked through the forest, whispers of peace,
The burden of his fears momentarily ceased.

I spoke of courage, of love's tender grace,
Of finding one's path in a bewildering space.
He listened intently, absorbing each word,
A flicker of light in his eyes, I observed.

I told him of strength found in darkest nights,
Of how we can rise, even from great plights.
He was just a young boy, no older than eight,
But in that moment, we shared our fate.

I showed him my life, the joys and the gains,
The love I'd found despite all the pains.
His tears began to dry, his face showed a smile,
Understanding that this struggle was worthwhile.

When I awoke, the memory stayed,
A reminder of the bond we'd made.
I dreamt a dream last night,
One of hope and endless light.

How They Choose Love

they choose.
they choose.
they choose.

not the love that cradles,
but the love that cuts.
not the love that stays,
but the love that lingers like smoke in their lungs.

they cup their hands around dying embers,
call it warmth.
they drink saltwater,
call it devotion.
they kneel before an altar of broken glass,
call it respect.

because love, to them,
is a moth circling a lightbulb,
thinking it has found the moon.

because love, to them,
is a lock clicking shut,
mistaking the weight of chains for the weight of arms
wrapped.

because love, to them,
is a ferris wheel with no exit,
spinning the same cycles,
always believing the next rotation will bring them somewhere
new.

but it never does.

still, they stay.
they grip the hands that tremble,
kiss the mouths that taste like ash,
fall asleep next to ghosts wearing familiar faces.

because what if love is supposed to hurt?

because someone, somewhere, once told them
that fire is the price of feeling something real.

and so they learn.
they learn that love is a storm,
and kindness is the eerie silence before it.

they learn that love must ache to be true.
so they flinch at gentleness, mistake patience for distance.

they learn that love must leave before it can be missed.
so they chase, they plead, they shrink.

they learn that love must break before it blooms.
so, they pick the hands that drop them first, mistake chaos for
chemistry.

they learn that love must be earned.
so they barter, they bleed, they beg.

they choose.
they choose.
they choose.

but what if—
just this once,
they didn't?

what if love was soft?
what if love did not ask them to break?
what if love was not a lesson in endurance?

would they even know what to do with it?

or would they turn away,
heart trembling,
hands empty,
lungs full of ghosts.

and whisper—
this is not for me.

Give The Crow Some Damn Water

Oh, sir, why did you end our agreement?

I hear the crows crowing at my door
An end to vitality forevermore.
A deathly youth that croaked out of spite
every night before I closed my eyes.

A repetitive crow that kills my seed.
A predictable gnarl of harsh hands
that refuse to feed me, refuse to feed.
Now that I drink out the marshlands,
A dirty water that fills my lungs,
But I drank this water when I wanted fun.

The taste of it bitter, yet still I consumed,
Ignoring the signs that our love was doomed.
What once was sweet now poisoned the well,
In this stagnant pond where we both fell.

Oh, sir, why did you end our vow?
Was it me that broke us, somehow?
The crows, they circle, but I still stand,
With filthy water and empty hands.

End of Agreement

Section 1: Terms of Separation
Herein lies the termination
Of vows spoken in softer years—
The warmth of whispered promises,
Now dissolved in frozen tears.

Clause 1.1: Division of Assets
The house, now hollow,
Shall be split in halves—
Bricks once built with hope
Reduced to scattered paths.

Clause 1.2: Custody of Memories
Photographs to be torn apart;
your smile's paint, a work of art,
my shadow faint, a fading trace
of laughter, time cannot replace.

Section 2: Grounds for Dissolution
The cold seeped in,
A breach of trust unspoken—
Our union once a fortress,
Now only stands broken.

Clause 2.1: Irreconcilable Differences
We spoke in words of ice,
Frostbite on every phrase.
No warmth remained to thaw
What love could not erase.

Clause 2.2: Emotional Withdrawal
I withheld affection;
You withdrew your heart—
A mutual exit from

Where we once did start.

Section 3: Finality of Agreement
Effective immediately,
The love that lingered, now nullified—
Here signed in ink,
Our final sigh, a silent goodbye.

Clause 3.1: Non-Renewal
This contract shall not be amended,
No appeal to be filed.
What was once a shared endeavor
Is now a distant, empty mile.

Clause 3.2: Penalties for Sentimentality
Should one of us remember
A touch too soft, a look too kind,
We forfeit the right to grieve—
Nostalgia's not part of this bind.

Signature: Two Names Scribbled
We hereby agree
To walk as strangers,
Love no longer owed—
This is the end of agreement.
Both parties have grown cold.

Memories on FIRE

It wasn't even ours—
not our spark, not our fault,
but still,
our lives were set alight.

**FLAMES LIKE TEETH,
JAWED AND RAVENOUS,
BITING THROUGH BEAM AND BRICK,
CONSUMING WITHOUT PAUSE, WITHOUT
MERCY.**

Nine years gone,
no longer home, but still home,
still where the roots held tight within the walls.

I wasn't there to mourn with you,
to sift through the charred remains of our memories,
my hands clean while yours blackened,
and I feel it,
the weight of everything that couldn't be saved.

**AND THE ROOF CAVED, THE WINDOWS
SCREAMED,
THE PAST CRACKED IN ITS FRAME,
SHRIVELING,
A PHOTO CURLED IN THE HEAT, A NAME
ERASED BY FIRE.**

In the flicker of flames,
the echoes of laughter slipped into smoke,
a graduation cap that once kissed the air,
now dust, like a neglected fire,
and diplomas—names burned, knowledge erased
but not the pride we held in those hands.

The old toys that lined the closet shelves,
they were relics of another time,
and now,
gone without a word,
gone without even the chance to say goodbye.

**WOOD SNAPS LIKE A SPINE,
SHINGLES TUMBLE LIKE FALLEN STARS,
AND THE WALLS—THOSE WALLS—
GASP, *SHRIEK*, <u>C O L L A P S E</u>**.

It was never about the things,
never the medals, the papers, the photographs,
but the space,
the air that held our breaths,
that housed our lives like a gentle cocoon.
How can we reclaim what the fire has claimed?

I couldn't be there,
to brush the ash from your hair,
to dig through the ruins,
to say, *we'll rebuild.*
But what is left to rebuild when all we've known is gone?

I dream of the walls we touched,
the couch where we sat in silence and in laughter.
These things, now shapeless, formless,
all lost to the flames that were never ours to light.

BUT KNOW THIS—
I carry it still,
even from a distance,
the warmth of what we were,
before the fire took it all away.

Third Face

In dark halls creep a
third face of mine that whispers,
"Who are you to speak?"

Malfeasance

Malfeasance, or am I just a lone man?
One who needn't useless smothering,
an endless tycoon of noxious mothering?
While others seemingly need hands held to stand?

Harsh I might be in words,
But loving at heart.
Overthink like Descartes,
Avoiding the herds.

My family is what I live for.
But my space is also needed.
So many arguments heated,
But home is no longer home for me.

Life is a tree of paths,
And I've branched off.
I'm growing into a being,
hopeful and anxious, awed and flawed.

Mr. Bee

I sit aloft over an overflowed swimming pool.
Just dreaming to jump in.
When, Mr. Bee, I saw you flapping your arms,
Begging me to come in.
Not for the fun of it, but because you were
drowning.

Shit.

I sit there numbly watching you suffer.
As if my mind needed to buffer.
Buzz, buzz, you flutter
Ten seconds, you lost all color.

Fuck.

Now your lifeless body just floats around.
One less bee for the world to deal with.
Except for the pool boy,
A person for you to make peace with.

But I continue to sit there,
a pain washing over me.
A guilt swashing over me.
And now I just watch your lifeless body.

What could I have done different?
Could I have saved your life?
I doubt you'd ever fly again,
But are your wings worth your life?

And what makes my life worth more than yours?
And vice-versa, for that matter?
That's not the question I should be asking,

why couldn't I take a single second
to give your life another chapter?

Instead, I sat there,
watching you throw your hands out,
begging for help.

But let's be honest,
if the tables were turned,
Would you do the same for me?
Even with your small hands,
Would you try?
Does it even matter if you'd try?
Am I obligated to die
Just because I was too lazy to try?

Fuck, I fucked up.

Sorry, Mr. Bee,
I shouldn't have been a coward.
I'm sorry you had to be my lesson,
And now my taste is left soured.
And your life devoured.

Warpaint

The twilight haze beats down on our backs.
My comrades, on their knees and heels,
Some keel over before being killed.
Athens and Sparta, a blood-soaked sweep,
A creep from death that dances over bodies that sleep.
No sound in the air except the breath I breathe.

Then I hear the ringing
RINGING RINGING **RINGING**
Of blades and shields and death-singing,
Earth-quaking, screams of my comrades.

Arrows harmoniously scream
through the night skies dark veil,
Ripping through the cries of man, the wails.
Each strike a tale of what might've been,
But we continue on, no way to win.

The dirt drinks the blood, a vampiric beast,
Sand is crimson, the souls released,
And in the wake of its endless feast,
Our strength awakens, not deceased.

Rain starts to rain, washing away
the blood from my hands, the blood
from the lands, the dirt, and crimson sands.

The warpaint washes down my face.
Appearing as black tears, mixed with my fears.
They tear through the fears and rants.
Until I have the want to fight to last man.

A Garden, a Fire

I smell the rich stench of burning
wood. I stand aloft amongst a beautiful
meadow. Is this the truth to rusted
adulthood? A wondrous garden that refuses to
grow?

So much potential in the beauty I
see. Yet we've let it go to
waste. We didn't stop to water the
seeds, and now the weeds are up to our
waist.

In the forest, when there's a
fire, it burns everything in its
path. But after, a sight to
admire, a place for nature to grow
back.

You can say I have a god
complex, but I took nature into my own
hands. I've destroyed everything,
and left nothing to our
plans.

I've committed this
atrocity because I love our
gardens. I mean no
animosity, nor do I expect a
pardon.

I am burning with my plants, too.
I am scorched like the earth,
the crackle of fire a song to dance to.
But with it, I hope for a place of rebirth.

Unclothed

I, bare skin against the night,
Fingers tremble, room too bright.
Your gaze like fire, burning slow,
I want to tell you, words won't flow.

An anxious dance, an aching trance,
caught 'tween fear and sweet romance.
Your lips, they graze, a sudden start,
to rip apart what's in my heart.

A sigh, a moan, the silence breaks,
Heat of bodies, the past mistakes.

The hands search, exploring fast,
Fear creeps in, shadows cast.
I've been alone, worn this mask.
Now unclothed, I don't dare ask:
Are you gentle, are you kind?
Detrimental, left behind?
Your touch is soft, but stings beneath,
The sweat, the breath, the tangled sheets,
The rhythm of hearts, the skipped heartbeats.

Still, we move in this cyclical race,
Chasing something that won't stay placed.
A flash, a grip, my fingers slip,
But I pull you in, our hearts skip.
I tremble, I crave, I fear the fall,
But here I am, unclothed, and all.

a weight lifted - in nine poems

i.
your sorrow
spills into my chest,
a river
that knows no borders.
my ribs ache
not from my pain
but yours.

ii.
how strange it is,
this human thing,
to hurt for wounds
that are not my own,
to carry scars
i did not earn.

iii.
you cried for hours
while i held the silence.
and though your tears
never touched my skin,
i felt them soak
my very soul.

iv.
we speak no words.
yet your gaze whispers:
i am seen.
in that moment
the weight of the world
feels lighter.

v.
empathy is not
an act of kindness;
it is survival.
a bridge we build
so we do not fall
into our own loneliness.

vi.
some say
the heart is fragile.
but how can that be
when it bends,
when it stretches
to hold so many lives
besides its own?

vii.
i cannot fix you.
but i can hold
the shattered pieces
until you are ready
to pick them up.

viii.
i have learned
the more i give,
the more i have
to give.
it is not depletion.
it is abundance.

ix.
your pain,
my pain—
it is the same.
perhaps this is why
we feel so much.
we are not separate.
we are threads
of the same tapestry.

Christian Gonzales

The Clumsy Watch-Bearer

I sit at the pier's rough wooden end,
feet tracing circles in the air.
A man stands beside me,
old fingers trembling, holding a pocket watch.

Tick, tick—
it ticks like it always had,
until it didn't.
It slipped from his hands,
dropped like a whisper,
swallowed by the sea.

I watch it fall,
slow and silent—
sinking, sinking.
Time dissolving into the deep.

He doesn't look at me.
Just stares down at the water,
as if waiting for God to reach in and return it.
But no hand came.

Tick, tick.

I hear it still,
or maybe I just imagine it.

"Was He watching?" I ask.
The man doesn't answer.

His silence like the sea.
They say He built it all,
crafted each cog,
each turning wheel,

every second of life.
Set it into motion,
and then what?
Did He lose it, too?

The watchmaker, blind—
perfect?
Hardly.
Just human,
like you, like me,
fumbling with time and hands too frail.

Tick, tick.

Maybe He's out there,
on another pier,
watching something else slip through His fingers.

Maybe the world's just a pocket watch,
dropped long ago.
And I sit here,
waiting for it to resurface,
but it never does.

Tick, tick.

Or does it?
And if He set it all in motion,
why does it wobble so?

Why does the world spin so crooked,
why do hearts stop too soon?
Is He out of sync?
Did He lose His tools?
Did He forget how it all works?

Tick, tick.
I wonder—
if He made us,
then why so many cracks?
Why this ticking beneath our skin,
that never quite aligns?
What kind of watchmaker makes something
that breaks so easily?

Tick, tick.

Was He distracted?
Or careless?
Or tired?
Maybe He never intended perfection,
maybe we are just experiments,
watches thrown together
in a cluttered workshop,
timepieces with bent gears,
tick-tocking our way to the end.

And if He's up there,
what's He doing now?
Sipping tea,
fiddling with another creation,
letting us rust in the rain?

Tick, tick.

The sound's growing louder.
Does He hear it?
Does He even care?
Or has He moved on,
left us here to wind down alone?

I look at the man beside me,
still staring at the water.

Has he accepted it,
the silence of the sea,
the absence of return?

Tick, tick.

And I wonder:
Does the watch even matter?
Do we matter?
Or are we just ticking away,
waiting for a moment
that never arrives?

Tick, tick.

Is He clumsy,
or deliberate?
A genius,
or a fool?
I wonder—
if we're broken,
are we broken by design?
Does He laugh at our stumbles,
or weep at our fall?

Tick, tick.

The man turns to leave,
and I stand up,
feeling the weight of that watch,
still ticking in the deep.

Maybe we'll never know
what the watchmaker meant.
Maybe we're just cogs in a machine
he forgot to oil,

or maybe we're meant to break,
to teach us to build again.

Tick, tick.

I wonder—
if we could stop the watch,
if we could break free from the ticking,
would we?
Or are we so used to the sound,
we'd miss it when it's gone?

Tick, tick.

I look at the sky,
at the horizon,
at the man walking away.
And the watch keeps ticking,
even as it sinks deeper.

Tick, tick.
Tick, tick.

Maybe that's the answer.
Or maybe—
there is no watch at all.

The Tyrant

Under the weight of his shackles, in halls of unending affliction,
Bound by a father—not blood-born, but forged in the fires of cruel law—
Labored a boy in the shadows, where sunlight was lost to the stone-heaps.
Gripped by a tyrant unyielding, whose voice was a lash on the spirit,
Kept in the gloom of the quarry, he toiled as the empire grew joyous.
Day after day in the hollows, his hands broke the rock into fragments,
Hardened by years in the labor, his sinew grew taut as the iron,
Yet in his soul there was fracture, a youth that the darkness had stolen.

Gone were the echoes of laughter, like leaves torn away by the tempest,
Fled was the spring of his childhood, stripped bare by the winter's harsh fingers.
Tyrants may sit on their thrones high, adorned with the crowns of their power,
Yet it is fear they rely on, a mantle they wear in their glory.
Fear in the boy was their treasure, a strength that the ruler delighted,
"Boy," cried the emperor loudly, "your life shall be service and silence,
Born to be nothing, forgotten, your end in the dungeon awaits

you."
Chains that he bound on those wrists there were forged not
of metal alone, but
Wrought in the depths of the psyche, a prison no key could
unfasten.

Still in the chest of that captive, a spark like the ash of a
bonfire
Glowed through the soot of his torment, an ember no lash
could extinguish.
Softly it flickered at first there, then swelled with each blow
that descended,
Burning within his deep heart-space, though none saw its light
in his features.
Years in the dust he endured then, with others who shared in
his burden,
Carving the stones till the daylight would sink to the edge of
the heavens.
Yet in the dusk of those evenings, when comrades lay broken
and weary,
He with a stone and a blade-edge—his own—honed the craft
of his vengeance.

Late in the stillness of midnight, he sparred with the shades of
old battles,
Thrusting his weapon at phantoms, till muscles cried out for
their respite.
Night after night he persisted, his sweat and his blood ran
together,
Sharpening steel and the fire that blazed in the core of his
being.
Tales of the bold he would murmur, of heroes who fell in

their honor,
Names like Prometheus carved he, their deeds in his mind
ever ringing—
Those who had shattered their fetters, defying the wrath of
the heavens,
Fought not for glory or scepters, but freedom, undying,
eternal.

Then came the dawn of his rising, from filth and the grime of
his prison,
Snapping the bonds on his forearms, with might that no iron
could hinder.
Loyal to none but his purpose, and those who had bled by his
side there,
Led he them forth from the shadows, a phoenix reborn in the
firelight.
Men from the fields he assembled, the lost and the crushed of
the empire,
Gave he them swords for their hands once deemed worthless
by lords of the palace.
Taught them the dance of the blade-edge, a master emerged
from a bondsman,
Forged he their anguish to power, till legions stood primed
for their justice.

Now on the plains soaked with crimson, where banners of
tyranny fluttered,
Hundreds arose in the moonlight, their armor agleam with
defiance.
Slaves once, now shadows of warcraft, united as kin in their
purpose,
Marched they to gates of the stronghold, to rend down the

walls of their despot.
Under the cloak of the night-sky, through valleys and fields they advanced then,
Silent, save breath of their lungs and the pulse of their hearts beating fiercely.
Far in the dark shone a torchlight, the palace a beacon of splendor,
Yet to the hero it whispered of weakness, a prize to be shattered.

"Onward," he breathed to his warriors, "the hour of freedom approaches,
Now we reclaim what was taken, our lives and our fates intertwined here.
Strike for the years of our torment, for chains that we bore in his service,
Strike for the blood that was spilled there, for nights when we begged for salvation."
Over the ramparts they clambered, their faces as still as the graveyards,
Cutting through sentries unyielding, till halls of the palace stood open.
Torches they bore like the starlight, their shadows on marble unfurling,
Stormed they the chambers of grandeur, where slumbered the lord of their anguish.

There on a throne hewn of granite, amid all the gold of his riches,
Woke the emperor, startled, to find that his reign was unravelling.
Father in name, not in spirit, he cowered, a wretch in his

power,
Pleading for life as his empire bled out on the stones by his
bedside.
"Father," the hero spoke softly, his sword in the dim light
now gleaming,
"Fear was your gift to my childhood, now taste of its blade in
your own turn."
Stroke after stroke rang like thunder, through halls that had
echoed with terror,
Blood of the tyrant anointed the floor as his kingdom lay
broken.

Gone was the realm of deception, reduced to the dust of
remembrance,
Victory blazed like a wildfire, yet cold stood the hero in
silence.
Years of his wrath had consumed him, a flame in the dark of
his spirit,
Now it was spent, and the sword-weight he bore felt a
stranger's possession.

Ink & Blood

With a quill in my grip, I have bled through the dusk,
Through the coal-smoke of thought, through the guttering husk
Of a mind that contorts, that snarls, that slips,
That cracks like a rib, that unspools at the lips.

The ink—it congeals, it clots in the air,
It crawls down my fingers, it pools in despair.
The bones, they complain, they shriek through the skin,
As if writhing to flee, as if fighting within.

BLOOD SPITS. PALMS BURN. WORDS SWELL. PAGE TURNS.
The vellum resists, yet it drinks what I've torn.
Each couplet—a wound, each line, a regret,
Yet the sentence still festers, *I CANNOT FORGET.*

Should I pause, should I smother, should I silence its cries?
Let the chalk settle thick, let the cobwebs baptize?
Or will pausing just widen the wound in my chest,
Let the ink tendril out, let it feast unaddressed?

The letters disfigure, but the story still breathes,
And the parchment devours, and the pen never leaves.
I am scrawling my ribs, with my knuckles laid bare,
But I cannot go back, I am already there.

FLESH FRACTURES. SPINE CURVES. EYES STING. WORDS SERVE.
The narrative slits, but the inkline still swerves.
For the scribe, the betrayer, the one who still bleeds,
Knows the story demands what the body concedes.

With a quill in my grip, I have bled through the dusk,

Through the coal-smoke of thought, through the guttering husk
Of a mind that contorts, that snarls, that slips,
That cracks like a rib, that unspools at the lips.

The Artist's Resurrection

You.
Yes, you.
Do you hear it?
The scratching beneath the floorboards,
the whisper in the dust?
They buried me in marble, sealed me in stone,
but ink does not decay,
and my brush still moves.

I was a name once.
A hand that shaped heavens in color,
that dragged gods from the void
and fixed them to ceilings.
They called me master, genius, saint,
and still, they let me rot.

But art—ha! Art is no gentle thing.
It will not sleep,
it will not kneel,
it will not go quietly into cracked frescoes
and forgotten halls.

So now, I rise.

Do you see?
The dust curls in swirls of vermilion and gold.
The wind hums in cadences I once knew.
My fingers, brittle as candle-wick,
find their form in the hush of canvas.
Even now, even now—
the paint does not dry.

And you, standing there, watching,
hands unstained,

heart untested—
Will you waste what I have clawed my way back to claim?

Pick up the brush.
Steady your hand.
Drag the world into light before they bury you too.

Christian Gonzales

New Crib

The walls stand bare,
their chipped paint whispers of lives before,
the floor creaks beneath my weight,
like an old man chuckling at youth's mistakes—
no couch, no bed,
just echoes filling empty corners.

Yet here I am,
in this space that could hold all my regrets,
but still stretch wide enough
to cradle the wild, untamed dreams
I haven't quite caught yet.

The fridge hums nervously,
the windows shiver when the wind passes through,
but I stand barefoot on cold tiles,
feeling every chill, every crack beneath me—
and it feels like a promise of something more.

Memories linger in the air,
fading like the dust floating in sunlight—
I breathe them in deep,
but exhale them gently,
letting go of what was.

This slum,
this crooked little space,
is nothing more than a canvas,
waiting for color to drip from my hands,
waiting for the strokes of what's to come.

The future hides in the plaster,
in hues I've yet to imagine—
but I will,

piece by piece,
as the days stretch on.

Tomorrow, perhaps, a plant.
Next week, maybe a chair.
But tonight, I'll sit on this cold floor,
laugh at the silence that wraps around me,
and toast to the wild, chaotic potential
of what this place,
and what I,
will grow to be.

My new crib—
a little rough, a little raw,
but bursting with room
for more.

The Sun Itself

Begin each morning as if the sun itself

has asked you to rise—not from sleep,

but from the pettiness of yesterday.

What is anger but fire burning its own shelter?

What is resentment but a storm summoned

only to drown in its rain?

I do not need their approval,

their apologies, their recognition.

I have this breath, this moment, this life.

The stars demand no gratitude for their light.

The earth asks nothing for the ground beneath us.

Why, then, should I demand from those

who stumble beside me?

Let me meet the world as it is,

and rise as it falls.

I Am Enough

I've spent years looking for cracks,
Tracing lines in the mirror like fault lines—
Thinking any moment now, I'd break,
Shatter into someone I wasn't supposed to be.
I've been the sculptor and the clay,
Chiseling at myself, trying to carve away
The pieces that didn't fit,
The flaws that refused to be smoothed out.

I was never enough,
Or so I told myself in whispers
When no one was listening.
Not strong enough,
Not smart enough,
Not sharp enough to cut through
The expectations they laid on me,
Like chains I couldn't shake off.

I've walked through life
Like I was trespassing,
Like I didn't belong in my own skin.
But I've come to see that the cracks
Are where the light gets in.

I am not broken;
I am whole
In every jagged edge,
Every scar I've etched into my own heart
With words that weren't mine to carry.

I've learned that enough
Is not a place you arrive,
It's the breath you take in the morning

When the sun hits your face,
The weight of your own hands
Resting on your chest
And feeling your pulse,
Steady, despite it all.

I am enough
In the way the sea is enough for the shore,
How it crashes and pulls away,
Never quite staying,
Always moving,
But still, it is home for the sand.

I am the storm and the stillness,
The question and the answer,
And even when I doubt,
I am the whole damn sky.

I used to think I needed to be more,
To grow into someone else's dream,
To stretch myself thin enough
To cover the holes they saw in me.

But I've learned that the only one
I ever needed to be
Was myself,
With all my jagged edges
And unfinished lines.

I am enough,
Even when the world screams otherwise.
I am enough,
Even when my own mind whispers doubt.
I am the sum of everything I've been,
And all I will become,
And in this messy, imperfect whole—
I've found my worth.

I am enough,
Not because I have to be,
But because I choose to be.
Because I've walked through fire
And come out the other side,
Not unscathed,
But still standing.

SHORT STORIES

DITCH DAY

The night was a heavy fist, pressing me into the lumpy mattress of my bedroom in our rotting house on the fringes of Pagosa Springs. The clock on my nightstand glared a sickly green—3:19 a.m.—its digits a cruel reminder of the sleep that eluded me, a taunting specter that left my eyes burning and my mind a jagged swirl of half-baked fears and buried grudges. Moonlight stabbed through the window's splintered frame, painting the walls with a silver glow that revealed chipped paint and water stains, each blemish a marker of the years our lives had been unraveling.

I kicked off the flimsy blanket, its frayed edges useless against the frigid air seeping through the walls, and sat up, the mattress springs wailing like a kicked dog. My room was a shrine to neglect: a rickety bookshelf sagged under the bulk of comics I hadn't touched since I was twelve, their covers faded from sunlight; a desk drowned in crumpled algebra worksheets, empty soda cans, and a dog-eared copy of *The Outsiders* I'd meant to finish but never did; a Nirvana poster curled at the edges, Kurt Cobain's haunted gaze staring through me like he could see the mess inside. Downstairs, I knew Mom was sprawled across the couch, lost in the chemical fog of whatever pills she'd scavenged—Oxycontin, maybe, or the Valium she hid in the bathroom cabinet. The TV would be on, its blue flicker washing over the living room, where beer cans and cigarette butts formed a grim collage on the coffee table, her altar to oblivion.

I swung my legs over the bed's edge, the floorboards biting my bare feet with an icy sting, and shuffled to the bathroom. The light buzzed, a sickly yellow that cast my reflection in the smudged mirror like a stranger's portrait. My face was gaunt, shadowed by dark circles, my hair a tangled snarl that hadn't seen a brush in weeks. I twisted the faucet, the pipes rattling like they were choking, and splashed frigid water on my cheeks, the shock jolting me into a fleeting clarity. The towel was stiff, streaked with rust from the leaking sink, and I scrubbed it across my skin, the coarse fibers scraping my jaw. I lingered, staring into my own eyes, searching for a spark of the kid I'd been—before Mom's addiction swallowed her whole, before Dad traded us for a new wife and a kid who wasn't a reminder of his failures. Nothing stared back but exhaustion, a hollowed-out version of myself I barely recognized.

Back in my room, I slung my backpack over one shoulder and crept downstairs, each step a calculated move to avoid the floorboards that squealed like snitches. The living room was a tableau of ruin: Mom limp on the couch, her head tilted at an awkward angle, the TV blaring an infomercial about a knife set that could "slice through anything." Beer cans littered the coffee table, an ashtray overflowed with cigarette butts, and a half-drunk bottle of Jack Daniel's stood guard by her hand. Her chest rose and fell, a faint rhythm of survival, and I stood there, caught in a dull pang—not love, not anymore, but a remnant of the bond we'd had when she'd wake me with pancakes, her laugh a melody that filled this house. Now, she was a husk, and I was just the kid who wasn't enough for her to come back.

I shook off the double-edged memory and stepped outside. The mountain air hit like a slap, crisp and biting, carrying the scent of pine and frost from the San Juan peaks that cradled the town. Pagosa Springs stretched before me, a patchwork of weathered bungalows, cracked sidewalks, and the distant steam of hot springs rising like a promise unkept. The sky was a bruised purple, the sun a faint rumor struggling through the clouds, casting long shadows that danced across the gravel.

By the time I reached the chain-link fence bordering the football field, dawn was clawing its way up the horizon, painting the sky in streaks of amber and soot. Trenton and Damien were already there, lounging against the metal with the careless swagger of guys who'd never given a damn about rules. Trenton was a human tank, his buzz-cut head tilted back as he laughed, his broad shoulders radiating a cockiness that felt like he was auditioning for a role he hadn't earned. Damien was leaner, all sharp angles and restless energy, his dark hair falling into eyes that glinted with a mix of mischief and malice, like a coyote sizing up its next move. He flicked a cigarette butt into the dirt, watching it glow briefly before grinding it out with his boot, his movements deliberate, almost ritualistic.

I trudged up, hands jammed in my pockets, and Trenton spotted me first, his grin splitting wide like he'd just won a bet. "Well, holy shit, Cody, you look like you got dragged through a ditch. What's the deal, man?"

I leaned against the fence, the metal's chill seeping through my hoodie, and shrugged, my voice rough from lack of sleep. "Insomnia's fucking me up. Barely closed my eyes last night."

Damien smirked, sparking another cigarette with a flick of his Zippo, the flame briefly illuminating his sharp features. "When I can't sleep, I just jerk off. Puts you out like a light, no bullshit."

I snorted, rolling my eyes to mask the faint embarrassment. "Yeah, I'll add that to my bedtime routine, Dr. Dickhead."

Trenton cackled, the sound bouncing off the bleachers, and kicked a loose pebble into the grass. "You two are nasty. I sleep like a bear—out by nine, up at six. Dad says it's 'cause I'm built for the grind."

Damien exhaled a plume of smoke, his gaze drifting to the mountains, their peaks jagged against the sky. "Your dad's a corporate shill. Mine spent last night screaming at the

Nuggets game—chucked a bottle when they blew it. TV's got a crack now, but he's too cheap to replace it."

I shifted, their words stirring the sludge of my own family crap. "Mine's probably off playing perfect dad with his new kid in Durango. Sent me a text last week—'You good, bud?' Like that fixes jack."

Trenton's eyes lit up, eager to pivot the mood. "Speaking of weekends, my cousin rolled in from Denver on Saturday. Dude's a straight-up lunatic—dragged me to this dive bar off Main. Bartender didn't even blink, just slid us beers. I was four deep before some biker started staring me down like I stole his Harley."

Damien raised an eyebrow, his smirk laced with doubt. "You're so full of it, Trenton. You'd piss your pants if a biker looked at you sideways."

"Fuck you," Trenton shot back, puffing out his chest like a rooster. "I stared him down, and he bailed. I don't back down from nobody."

I smirked, jumping into the fray. "What, you flex your baby biceps at him? Scare him off with your acne?"

Trenton flipped me off, but his grin held, unbothered. "Keep talking, asshole. Least I've got stories. You just mope around watching *Scream* reruns all weekend."

"Nah," I said, scuffing my shoe against the dirt, kicking up a small cloud. "Caught *Friday the 13th* last night. Jason's still the king—no contest with this new jump-scare garbage."

Damien nodded, flicking ash into the breeze, his approval a rare currency. "Respect. Old-school horror's got balls, not like the PG-13 crap they churn out now."

The conversation bounced like a stray bullet, ricocheting through random corners. Trenton launched into a tirade about our math teacher, Mrs. Jenkins, who'd flunked him for not showing his work on a quiz. "Bitch thinks I'm gonna solve world hunger with algebra. X plus Y equals who gives a flying fuck?"

Damien laughed, a low, gravelly sound that cut through the morning air. "She's got a hard-on for failing you, man. Probably dreams about your F's."

I piled on, emboldened by their energy. "She caught me sketching in class once—tore up my drawing right in front of everyone. Said I'd be flipping burgers if I didn't 'apply myself.'"

Trenton threw his hands up, theatrical as hell. "They're all the same, I swear. Like, what's the point? We're not building rockets—we're just trying to get through this shithole without losing our minds."

We stood there, the talk sprawling like a wildfire, touching on everything from the local diner's greasy burgers to a rumor about a kid who got expelled for selling weed in the bathroom. Trenton swore he'd seen a coyote in his backyard last week, "big as a damn wolf," while Damien countered with a story about his neighbor's dog that got eaten by a mountain lion. I tossed in a half-assed tale about a hawk I'd seen circling over the hot springs, mostly to keep up, but my mind was elsewhere, snagged on the image of Mom's limp form on the couch, the way her hand twitched like she was reaching for something she'd never find.

The first bell screeched across the field, a shrill blade slicing through the dawn, and students started trudging toward the school's entrance—a sluggish parade of backpacks, hoodies, and glazed-over eyes. Damien stubbed out his cigarette on the fence, his face twisting into a scowl. "Another day in the meat grinder. I'm not sitting through Jenkins' algebra torture—she can shove her equations up her ass."

Trenton's eyes sparked, his voice dropping to a conspiratorial hush, like he was plotting a heist. "You thinking what I'm thinking, man?"

Damien's grin was slow and vicious, a predator scenting blood. "Ditch day, boys. Real men don't waste their lives on quadratic bullshit—let's own this fucking town."

My stomach lurched, a chaotic mix of thrill and dread surging through me like a rogue wave. "You guys are batshit. What if we get caught? My dad'll ground me 'til I'm collecting dust."

Damien's stare was a switchblade, cutting through my hesitation. "What, you gonna cry to Daddy? Grow some balls, Cody."

Trenton slapped my shoulder, his enthusiasm a freight train. "Don't be a wuss, man. We're gods today—untouchable. You in or out?"

I bit my lip, the faint taste of blood grounding me as I wrestled with the choice. Home was a dead end—Mom drowning in her pills, Dad a stranger with his new wife and kid, their perfect little life in Durango a world I'd never touch. School was just another trap, a conveyor belt to nowhere, with teachers like Jenkins who saw me as a lost cause. But here, with Trenton and Damien, I was somebody, a spark in their wildfire, a kid who could be more than the sum of his failures. The risk was a boulder in my chest, heavy with the promise of consequences—groundings, lectures, maybe worse. But the pull of their world, their reckless, living world, was stronger. "Alright," I said, my voice a shaky thread but resolute. "I'm in."

The second bell wailed, a banshee cry that set the hallway ablaze with chaos—lockers slamming shut, sneakers squeaking on linoleum, voices overlapping in a cacophony of teenage entropy. Trenton and Damien slipped into the crowd, their figures blurring toward the side exit, their laughter a faint, taunting call. I stood frozen, my heart pounding like a war drum, as kids shoved past, a river dragging me toward Mrs. Jenkins' classroom. Doubt crashed over me, cold and suffocating, a voice in my head screaming to turn back. *This is stupid. You're gonna get fucked. Walk away.* I took a step toward the classroom, my backpack dragging like a chain, my resolve crumbling like dry clay. Jenkins' door loomed just ahead, her pinched face waiting to drone on about variables and exponents, her chalkboard a prison sentence I'd serve for the next two hours.

But then I saw them—Trenton's red jacket flashing at the hallway's end, Damien's mocking grin as he glanced back, his eyes daring me to follow. They were free, cutting through the bullshit, living a story I'd only dreamed of. I was still here, stuck in the same tired script, a nobody fading into the background.

Fuck this. The thought was a spark, igniting a reckless fire in my veins. I spun on my heel, shoving through the crowd, my sneakers screeching as I sprinted. Lockers blurred past, a smear of red and gray, as I dodged a teacher's outstretched arm—"Hey, stop right there!"—and weaved around a kid lugging a trombone case. A janitor's mop bucket clattered as I clipped it, water splashing my jeans, but I didn't stop, my breath ragged, my pulse a frantic rhythm. Faces turned, mouths agape, but I was a bullet, unstoppable, tearing through the chaos with a wild, desperate joy.

I slammed into the side exit, the metal door crashing against the wall with a thunderous bang, and burst into the morning light. The mountain air hit like a shot of whiskey, crisp and exhilarating, flooding my lungs with freedom. I tore up the trail behind the school, legs pumping, lungs screaming, the dirt crunching beneath my sneakers like a battle cry. The world fell away—school, rules, the suffocating cage of my life—until it was just me, the slope under my feet, and the raw, electric pulse of being alive. I ran until my chest burned, until the school was a speck below, swallowed by the San Juan's jagged embrace, and I was no longer the kid who didn't matter.

I caught up to them at a boulder halfway up the trail, Trenton sprawled like a king surveying his domain, Damien pacing like a caged predator restless for the next hunt. Damien greeted me with a slow, sarcastic clap, his grin sharp and taunting. "Well, goddamn, the runaway makes it. Thought you'd be kissing Jenkins' ass by now, begging for mercy."

Trenton laughed, the sound ricocheting off the pines like a gunshot. "Yeah, dude, I had you pegged for a snitch, bawling, 'I'm so sorry, ma'am!'"

I doubled over, gasping, sweat dripping into my eyes, stinging like hell. "Screw you both," I panted, a grin breaking through despite myself. "I'm here, alright? Took my sweet time, but I'm here."

Damien's eyes flickered with something close to respect, a rare crack in his armor. "Alright, hero. Let's fucking roll."

The trail stretched ahead, a jagged scar cutting through the scrubby pines and rocky outcrops that flanked Pagosa Springs High, now just a smudge in the valley below. My sneakers crunched on the gravel, each step a pulse of freedom, my lungs still burning from the mad dash out of school. The San Juan Mountains loomed overhead, their peaks clawing at a sky streaked with clouds like torn cotton, the air sharp with the bite of frost and the faint tang of sap. Trenton lumbered beside me, his broad frame casting a shadow that danced across the dirt, while Damien prowled ahead, all lean menace and restless energy, his dark hair flapping like a tattered flag. We were outlaws now, unshackled from the grind of algebra and hall passes, and the thrill of it was a live wire in my veins, electric and dangerous.

We didn't talk much at first, just walked, the silence broken by the rustle of wind through the trees and the occasional hawk screeching above. My mind churned, replaying the sprint through the hallway—lockers blurring, the janitor's mop bucket splashing, the door slamming open to spit me into this new world. I'd almost chickened out, one foot in Jenkins' classroom, ready to slump into my usual desk and fade away. But I hadn't. I'd run, and that choice, that single reckless act, made me feel like I was more than the kid nobody noticed, the one whose mom was a junkie and whose dad had traded him for a shinier life in Durango.

Trenton broke the quiet, his voice booming like he was auditioning for a stage. "My cousin was telling me about this party in Durango last month—total chaos. Some dude got so wasted he passed out in the pool, just floating like a dead trout. Cops showed up, and everyone bolted."

Damien snorted, kicking a loose rock that skittered down the path. "Your cousin's a bullshit artist. Probably made it up to sound like a big shot."

"Nah, man, he's the real deal," Trenton insisted, undeterred, his buzz-cut head bobbing with conviction. "Said there was this chick doing body shots off the DJ's turntable. I'm crashing that scene when I'm older, no question."

I stayed quiet, my thoughts snagging on the weekend I'd spent holed up in my room, Mom comatose on the couch, the house silent except for the TV's endless drone. "I just watched some old kung fu flicks," I said finally, scuffing my shoe against a root. "Bruce Lee's still a badass—*Enter the Dragon* kicks the shit out of anything new."

Damien nodded, his lips curling in rare approval. "Solid pick."

The trail curved, and we stumbled on a power substation, its skeletal transformers hunched behind a rusted chain-link fence, their hum a low, angry buzz like a nest of hornets plotting revenge. We stopped, drawn to the eerie sound, the air around it thick with the smell of ozone and scorched metal. The fence was dented in places, tagged with faded graffiti—initials, a crude middle finger, a heart with a knife through it. Trenton squinted, hands on his hips, his broad frame blocking the sun. "What the hell's this thing? Sounds like it's gonna explode."

Damien's eyes sparked, that wild glint he got when he was about to spin a yarn. He leaned in, voice dropping to a conspiratorial rasp. "Government shit, man. They're pumping mind-control waves into town, zapping our brains to make us obedient little drones for their new world order."

Trenton's jaw dropped, his eyes wide as hubcaps. "No fucking way. That's some *X-Files* shit right there."

I rolled my eyes, skepticism warring with my instinct to avoid Damien's temper. "Sounds like you swiped that from a comic book, dude."

He spun on me, his stare sharp enough to cut glass. "You calling me a liar, Cody? Open your damn eyes—they've got us tagged like lab rats."

Trenton jumped in, nodding like a bobblehead on a dashboard. "My uncle saw a UFO once—hovered right over his barn, lights flashing and everything. Bet it's all tied to this."

I sighed, letting it drop. Damien's conspiracies were a brick wall, and banging my head against them was a losing game. "Whatever."

We circled the fence, tossing rocks at the transformers, the clangs ringing out like off-key bells. Trenton started ranting about a sci-fi movie he'd seen, something about aliens melting brains with lasers. "Sickest scene ever—dude's head just pops like a zit."

Damien smirked, lobbing a stone that sparked against the metal. "Sounds fake as hell. Real aliens would just nuke us and be done with it."

I leaned against a tree, the bark rough under my palms, and stared at the humming towers, their drone sinking into my bones. It reminded me of the static in my head when I lay awake, the endless mill of thoughts I couldn't shut off. "You ever wonder what's out there?" I asked, half to myself, my voice barely carrying over the buzz. "Like, beyond Pagosa, beyond all this?"

Trenton shrugged, chucking another rock. "Yeah, but who cares? I'm just trying to score a truck and a girlfriend, you know?"

Damien's grin faded, his voice low, almost raw. "Out there's just more pricks like my dad, beating on you for breathing. Better to stay here, make our own rules."

I met his eyes, catching a flicker of something real beneath the bravado. Then Damien turned, spitting into the dirt. "Come on, let's bounce."

The trail twisted downward, spitting us out at the edge of the town cemetery, a sprawling mess of crooked tombstones and tangled weeds that smelled of damp earth and rot. The sky had darkened, clouds piling up like a bruise, and the air hung heavy, pressing against my skin. Damien vaulted the rusted fence with a whoop, strutting among the graves like he was king of the underworld. Trenton scrambled after, his laughter jarring against the silence, a bullhorn in a library. I hesitated, a chill slithering up my spine, the sight of all those stones stirring a memory of my uncle's funeral years ago—Mom sobbing, her hands shaking as she clutched a crumpled tissue, me too young to understand why she was breaking. I shook it off and climbed over, the metal bar cold and gritty under my hands, landing with a thud on the other side.

We wandered through the maze of headstones, some so weathered the names were gone, others cracked like they'd been kicked. Damien launched into a ghost story, his voice low and dramatic, like he was auditioning for a campfire. "Heard about this grave-robbing crew back in the '80s, right here in Pagosa. Dudes were digging up bodies, selling 'em to some sketchy doctor in Durango for experiments. One night, they say a corpse sat up and screamed, eyes glowing red."

Trenton's eyes bugged out, his mouth half-open. "No fucking way. That's some zombie apocalypse shit."

I smirked, but my skin prickled, the story hitting too close to the unease already crawling through me. "Probably just drunk kids making it up to scare people."

Damien shot me a look, his lips curling. "You're no fun, Cody. What's your deal—scared of a little spooky?"

"Nah," I said, kicking a pebble that bounced off a stone. "I just don't buy every wild tale you pull out of your ass."

Trenton cut in, pointing to a faded marker half-buried in weeds. "My grandpa's around here somewhere. Kicked it before I was born—Vietnam vet, drank himself blind. Mom says he was a hero, but I think he was just a guy who got screwed by life."

Damien's face hardened, his voice flat, a rare slip in his usual swagger. "Mine's still kicking, worse fucking luck. Smacked me last week over a slice of leftover pizza. Worthless bastard."

I glanced at him, startled by the rawness, the way his eyes flicked away like he'd said too much. "That why you're always out here, dodging the bus home?"

He bristled, his stare a warning flare. "Don't play shrink, Cody. You don't know shit about my life."

We found a low stone wall, its surface pitted and mossy, and sat, the cold seeping through my jeans. The silence stretched, heavy, until I rubbed my eyes, yawning.

The mood shifted, and we started tossing pebbles at a broken angel statue, its wings chipped, its face blank. Trenton rambled about a horror game he'd played, something about zombies in a mall, while Damien countered with a story about a haunted cabin his cousin swore he'd seen near the hot springs. I didn't say much, my mind drifting to that funeral again, Mom's sobs, the way she'd clung to me like I was her lifeline, only to let go in the years since. The cemetery felt like a mirror, all these stones marking lives that ended, dreams that fizzled out, and I wondered if that's what waited for me—a name on a slab, forgotten.

Damien stood, pacing, his restlessness infectious. He stopped at a grave, a newer one with fresh dirt, and started humping the air above it, laughing like a hyena. "Teabag city, boys! Who's got the balls to join me?"

Trenton unzipped, pissing on a headstone with a gleeful whoop, the stream glinting in the dim light. "Take that, grandpa!"

Damien whipped his dick out and pissed on the slab with Trenton. He turned to me, his grin a taunting crescent. "Don't be a fag, Cody. Get in on this."

My face burned, a mix of disgust and humiliation churning in my gut. The image of Mom at that funeral flashed again, her grief raw and real, and I couldn't shake it. "That's fucked up, man," I said, my voice steady despite the heat in my cheeks. "I'm not pissing on someone's grave."

Trenton fastened his jeans, his smirk unrelenting. "What, your dick too tiny? Bet it's a fucking acorn."

Damien's laughter sliced through me, sharp and mean. "Yeah, a goddamn tic-tac—microscopic!"

I clenched my fists, my pulse hammering. "Eat shit, both of you. I've got some fucking standards."

Damien shrugged, his interest fading as he sauntered off. "Suit yourself, choirboy."

We wandered deeper, the graves blurring together, the town nowhere in sight. My stomach knotted as I realized we were lost, the paths twisting back on themselves. Trenton squinted, pointing downhill. "Town's that way, right?"

Damien cursed, his patience fraying. "Fuck it—we're cutting through Carver's land."

My heart lurched, dread pooling like oil. "Old Man Carver? Guy's unhinged—he'll shoot us dead!"

Trenton puffed out his chest, bravado in overdrive. "We're too quick for that fossil. Let's roll."

Damien was already moving, his strides purposeful. "Stop whining, Cody. Hustle your ass."

The hill sloped toward Carver's property, a wooded stretch with a sagging cabin tucked among the pines, its perimeter bristling with barbed wire. The air was thicker here, heavy with the scent of damp bark and something sour, like rotting leaves. We stopped at the fence, its metal glinting dully under the overcast sky, and argued, our voices low but heated. Damien spun a tale about a kid who'd vanished on Carver's land years ago, "probably buried under the shed," his eyes glinting with dark amusement. Trenton called it bullshit but admitted he'd heard Carver once shot a dog for sniffing his trash. I stood back, my pulse racing, the stories piling up like storm clouds. "This is a bad idea," I said, my voice tight. "He's not just some crank—he's dangerous."

Damien sneered, already climbing the fence, his boots scraping the wire. "Don't be a pussy, Cody. You wanna walk ten miles around? Move it."

Trenton followed, his bulk making the fence wobble, and I stood there, my hands clammy, my mind screaming to turn back. But they were over, tearing downhill, their laughter fading into the trees, and I was alone, the cemetery behind me, the town a distant dream. *Don't choke. Don't be that kid.* I grabbed the wire, the barbs pricking my palms, and hauled myself over, landing hard on the other side, my breath hitching. The hill was steep, dotted with rocks and gnarled roots, and I started running, my sneakers slipping on the damp earth, trying to catch them.

The cabin door slammed open, a gunshot crack that froze my blood. Old Man Carver stormed out, shotgun cocked, his face a mask of rage carved from years of solitude. "What the fuck you little shits doing on my land? I'll blow your goddamn heads off!"

Trenton and Damien ducked behind a cluster of pines, their forms swallowed by the shadows. I was caught in the open, a deer in the crosshairs, my heart hammering so loud I thought it'd burst. My mind scrambled, panic clawing at me. *Lie—say something, anything.* I raised my hands, trembling, my voice wobbly but desperate. "Sir, I'm so sorry—my mom's in the hospital. Got a call in town—car accident. This was the fastest way through, I swear."

Carver's barrel wavered, his eyes narrowing to slits, weathered lines deepening around them. "Hospital? What happened to her?"

"Bad wreck," I blurted, the lie spilling out like water from a busted dam. "She's in surgery. Might not make it. I'm just trying to get there."

He studied me, the shotgun still raised but less steady, his scowl softening just a hair. "Hell of a thing, kid. Hope she pulls through. Get moving—and don't let me catch you here again, you hear?"

I nodded, a marionette jerked by relief, and bolted, my legs shaky as I stumbled downhill. I found Trenton and Damien behind a boulder, their faces a mix of awe and amusement. Trenton's jaw hung loose. "Dude, what'd you tell him?"

I panted, my chest heaving, the adrenaline still spiking. "Told him my mom's dying in a hospital. Bought it hook, line, and sinker."

Damien laughed, a sharp bark, and smacked my back, his hand heavy. "You cunning son of a bitch! That's some Oscar-level con artistry right there."

I forced a grin, their praise a rush that lit me up, but the lie twisted in my gut like a knife. Mom wasn't in a hospital bed—she was wasting away on our couch, probably hadn't moved since I left. I'd used her, turned her pain into a get-out-of-jail-free card, and the guilt of it was a splinter I couldn't pull out. But Damien's hand on my shoulder, Trenton's wide-eyed respect—it felt like belonging, like I was finally part of their world, and that high was worth the sting.

The trail spilled us into the ragged heart of Pagosa Springs, where the town's edges frayed like a worn-out shirt, all chipped paint and sagging porches under the San Juan Mountains' unyielding gaze. Dusk was creeping in, the sky a smear of indigo and ash, the air turning sharp with the promise of night. My sneakers dragged on the cracked asphalt, each step heavier than the last, the adrenaline from Carver's shotgun showdown fading into a jittery hum. Trenton lumbered beside me, his broad frame casting a shadow that swallowed the sidewalk, while Damien prowled ahead, his lean silhouette cutting through the twilight like a blade. We were still high on the day's chaos—ditching school, defying graves, outsmarting a crazy old man.

We veered toward the abandoned market, a hulking relic on the town's edge, its walls scarred with graffiti and broken windows gaping like missing teeth. The sign above—*Pagosa Market, Est. 1972*—was faded, half the letters gone, and the parking lot was a graveyard of shattered bottles and cigarette butts. Damien beelined for the rusted ladder bolted to the side, climbing with the agility of a cat, his boots clanging on the metal rungs. Trenton followed, huffing as his bulk strained the frame, and I brought up the rear, my palms slick on the cold steel, the ladder creaking under each step.

We spilled onto the roof, a flat expanse littered with debris—empty beer cans, a shredded tire, a condom wrapper curling in the breeze. The air up here was cleaner, tinged with pine and the faint sulfur of the hot springs miles away, but the view was pure Pagosa: sagging rooftops, the ribbon of the San Juan River, and the mountains overlooking us, their peaks swallowed by clouds. We sprawled out, backs against the gravelly surface, bottles clinking under our elbows. The day's chaos felt distant up here, like we'd climbed into a pocket of the world where rules didn't exist.

Damien stretched, his smirk lazy and self-assured. "I've fucked so many chicks up here, man—Durango girls, hot as hell. Weed, whiskey, parties that'd blow your virgin minds."

Trenton's eyes popped, his jaw dropping like a cartoon. "No shit? You're a goddamn legend, Damien."

I nodded, half-convinced, my voice cautious. "Sounds pretty wild."

Damien sat up, his stare piercing, like I'd insulted his bloodline. "You doubting me, Cody? I'm the fucking king of this roof—ask anyone."

Trenton leapt to his defense, eager as a puppy. "Bet you've got bitches lined up, like a pimp running a club."

"Abso-fucking-lutely," Damien crowed, his ego ballooning. "You two wouldn't get it—still yanking it to your mom's Cosmo stash."

I snorted, picking at a loose shingle, the rough texture grounding me. I'd never even held a girl's hand, let alone anything close to Damien's tall tales, but I wasn't about to admit it. Trenton kept the ball rolling, his voice thick with bravado. "My military brother hooked up with this chick when he was based in Germany—total freak. Sent me a pic once, tits like you wouldn't believe."

Damien scoffed, tossing a bottle cap that glinted as it spun. "Military's for drones. I'd rather slit my wrists than salute some asshole in a uniform."

I stared at the horizon, the mountains a dark silhouette against the fading light, and let my thoughts spill out. "I'd enlist just to get the hell out of Pagosa. Anywhere's better than this dead-end town."

Trenton blinked, caught off guard. "Your dad cool with that?"

"Doesn't give a damn," I said, the truth a bitter shard. "He's got his new wife, new kid—I'm just the fuck-up he left behind."

Damien's voice softened, a rare crack in his armor. "Families are a scam. We're our own crew—fuck the rest."

Our eyes locked, a fleeting moment of understanding, like we were all carrying the same bruise. Then he stood, dusting off his jeans, and started tossing bottles at a rusted vent, the glass shattering with satisfying pops. We joined in, the roof turning into our playground, our laughter sharp against the quiet. Trenton bragged about a party he'd crashed, claiming he'd outdrunk a college kid, while Damien spun a story about a street fight he "totally won" against some gangster in Albuquerque. I stayed quiet, my mind drifting to a night I'd tried talking to Mom about my dreams—music, maybe, or just getting out. She'd stared through me, her eyes glassy, and I'd walked away, the words dying in my throat.

The talk veered to music, a safer ground. Trenton swore by Metallica, banging his head to an imaginary *Master of Puppets*. Damien argued for Nirvana, claiming *Nevermind* was the rawest shit ever. I threw in Green Day, *Dookie*'s snotty energy my go-to when insomnia hit. We bitched about Pagosa's lack of a skate park, the shitty arcade that ate quarters, and the diner's burgers that tasted like cardboard. Up here, we were kings, untouchable, rewriting the rules of a town that didn't care.

Damien checked his phone, the screen's glow harsh in the dusk. "Bus is coming soon. Let's hit the road."

We climbed down, the ladder groaning under us, and cut through town, the streets quiet except for the hum of streetlights flickering on. We passed the community center, its windows fogged, the thump of music leaking out. A Zumba class was in full swing, middle-aged women in tight leggings bouncing to a Latin beat, their shadows swaying like a fever dream. We stopped, drawn like moths, our faces pressed to the glass, the warmth of our breath clouding the pane.

Trenton's eyes bulged, his voice a stage whisper. "Goddamn, check those MILFs! I'd plow every one of 'em."

Damien licked his lips, his grin pure sleaze. "Fuck yeah, I'd hit that 'til they're hobbling."

I laughed, caught up in the crude energy, but my stomach twisted, a faint unease I couldn't name. The male instructor inside caught us staring, his face breaking into a grin as he pointed at the women's curves, nodding like he was one of us. We hooted, hyped by the camaraderie—until his expression soured, his finger jabbing at the door, his lips mouthing a furious *Get the fuck out, you little shits!*

Damien doubled over, laughing so hard he wheezed. "What a fucking prick!"

Trenton clutched his sides, howling.

I forced a chuckle, but the humor curdled, leaving a residue of shame. Those women weren't just bodies—they were someone's moms, maybe like mine had been once, dancing in our kitchen to oldies, her smile bright before the pills stole it. I'd leered like they were nothing, and the realization felt like stepping in something foul.

Trenton nudged me, his brow creased. "You good, Cody? You're all quiet."

"Yeah," I lied, forcing a grin. "Just beat from running from Carver."

Damien rolled his eyes, his patience thin. "Always moping. Lighten up, you wuss."

We reached the middle school curb, the sky now a deep navy, stars prickling through the clouds. The streetlights cast a sickly yellow glow, and the air was cold, nipping at my exposed wrists. We sprawled on the concrete, backs against the curb, the day's buzz still humming in our bones. Trenton's face lit up, his voice buoyant. "We should start a band, dudes. Get a van, tour the country—leave this shithole in the dust."

Damien leaned in, his usual cynicism melting into a rare spark of hope. "Hell yeah—no more drunk dads, no more bitch principals. Just us, shredding stages, living like kings."

I nodded, tugging at my shoelaces, the vision taking root like a seed in cracked pavement. "That'd be fucking epic. Our rules, our world."

Trenton turned to me, eager. "You play guitar, right? What else you got?"

"Just that," I said, picturing Dad's old Stratocaster, gathering dust in the garage, its strings silent like his promises. "Could swipe it, start something real."

Damien clapped, his zeal contagious. "Then it's settled. Steal that bitch—we're on our way to glory."

We sat there, architects of a future we could almost touch, our voices drawing dreams as the town slept around us. Trenton swore we'd paint the van black, with flames on the sides, and play Metallica covers until our fingers bled. Damien wanted to hit Seattle, "where Kurt made history," and write songs that'd burn the world down. I saw us in dive bars, the crowd screaming our name, a life where I wasn't the kid who didn't matter. We griped about Pagosa's one-stoplight boredom, the way the mountains trapped us, but up here, on this curb, they felt like a challenge we could conquer.

The bus rumbled into view, its brakes hissing like a tired beast, its headlights cutting through the dark. We stood, dusting off our jeans, the dream lingering like smoke. I climbed on first, my stomach dropping as I spotted Maddie and Ellie—my stepsister and sister—in the back, their glares sharp enough to draw blood. Maddie's eyes narrowed, her voice a hiss. "You're so fucked, Cody. Dad's gonna skin you alive."

Ellie leaned forward, her sneer matching. "Yeah, dumbass, we heard you ditched. Good luck surviving this one."

I slumped into a seat, the vinyl cold and sticky, the day's exhilaration crashing like a wave against the shore of reality. Dad would know—grounding was the least of it. Maybe he'd drag me to Durango, force me to sit through another lecture about "responsibility" while his new kid toddled around, oblivious. But as the bus lurched forward, Pagosa Springs smearing past the window in a blur of streetlights and shadows, I clung to the ember of that day. I'd run, I'd lied, I'd stood my ground. I'd been alive, part of something bigger than the cage of my life, and that feeling—raw, electric, undeniable—was worth every damn consequence.

DUST

139 AD, Caelian Hill in Rome

Upon the Palatine's ascent, where the earth lies parched and unyielding, young Marcus Aurelius Verus, not yet burdened by the mantle of empire, trod with sandals that scraped against the arid soil, stirring motes of dust that clung to his shins like supplicants beseeching alms from a heedless lord. Below sprawled Rome, a labyrinth of crimson tiles and the raucous cries of corvids, where the Tiber's gleam dulled beneath a sun relentless in its dominion, as if the heavens themselves scorned respite. At seventeen summers, Marcus was a youth of slender frame and ceaseless queries, his dark locks curling in wild defiance of his aunts' decorum, his eyes—too wide for a visage yet softening from boyhood's tenderness—searching ever for truths beyond the poets' verses that filled his mind.

He hastened, for he was tardy, and Quintus Junius Rusticus, his tutor in the ways of reason, brooked no delay. A waxed tablet, its stylus pricking his side, hung heavy beneath his arm, the dampness of his tunic clinging to his neck as the slope's incline taxed his breath. His grandfather, Annius Verus, that stern patriarch whose voice rasped like a millstone, had dispatched him to Rusticus not for the boy's desire, but to scour the softness of poetry from his soul. "Thy head is overfull of Catullus' ardent kisses and Virgil's fields of honeyed bloom," the elder had growled, his words a cartwheel's rumble o'er gravel. "Rusticus shall forge thee into a man of substance, not a dreamer lost to verse." Marcus had held his tongue, as was his wont, for to contend with Annius was to challenge the tides.

The dwelling of Rusticus, though modest compared to the marble halls of his uncles' pride, stood resolute near the hill's summit, its walls stained ochre by the relentless dance of dust and rain through seasons uncounted. A slave, his nose bent as a shepherd's crook, ushered Marcus through the gate with a mutter scarce audible—"The master awaits in the garden." Adjusting the tablet, its edges biting his ribs, Marcus stepped into the shade of a fig tree, its boughs heavy with fruit gone soft and sour upon the earth.

There sat Rusticus, stooped o'er a table of weathered timber, his broad hands sifting scrolls as a farmer sorts grain from chaff. A man of perchance forty winters, yet his visage bore the furrows of three score, etched deep by the ceaseless observation of men's failings—their own, and those of Rome. His toga, unadorned and loose, lacked the starched pleats

Marcus' kin so prized, a garment suited to labour rather than parade. He did not raise his gaze. "Thou comest late, boy," he spake, his voice as unyielding as the flagstones of the Forum.

Marcus shifted, the tablet's weight a sudden burden, his tongue tasting the dust upon the air. "The Forum was thronged, master," he ventured, his words a frail offering. "A mule's leg did break nigh the Basilica Aemilia, and the throng held fast all passage." Truth it was, yet beneath Rusticus' unwavering stare, it felt a frail shield, as if the gods themselves might scorn such an excuse.

Rusticus grunted, rolling a scroll tight with a flick of his wrist, the papyrus crackling like dry leaves underfoot. "A mule's misfortune doth not govern thy steps, Marcus. Thine own will doth that." He gestured to a stool across the table, its wood worn smooth by years of such lessons. "Sit thee down."

Marcus obeyed, the stool groaning beneath him as he settled, the garden's air thick with the scent of withered thyme and the faint rot of fallen figs. A breeze stirred the leaves above, yet the heat pressed down, unyielding as a centurion's command. Rusticus slid a scroll toward him, its edges frayed as if gnawed by time. "Epictetus," he declared, voice a hammer upon anvil. "Read. Aloud."

Marcus unrolled the papyrus, his fingers unsteady, the Greek script a legion of letters marching in rigid order. He cleared his throat, voice faltering upon the first utterance. "That which lieth not within thy dominion to effect, seek not to desire..." A stumble, a glance upward—Rusticus' eyes, gray as the Tiber under storm, fixed upon him, unblinking as a hawk o'er its quarry.

"Proceed," Rusticus commanded, his tone a stone dropped into still waters.

"…for thou shalt be wretched and cast down in spirit," Marcus continued, the words a bitter draught upon his tongue. Epictetus spake of fetters and liberty, of what a man might grasp and what must needs slip through his fingers like sand. The prose was stark, unadorned—far from Virgil's hexameters that rolled as waves upon a shore. Marcus finished the passage, the scroll curling back upon itself as a serpent recoiling.

Rusticus leaned forth, his elbows upon the table, the wood creaking under his weight. "What meaning dost thou glean, boy?"

Marcus paused, his fingers tracing a splinter upon the stool, his mind a storm of thoughts unmoored. "That we ought not to yearn for what we cannot possess?" he ventured, voice a tentative whisper.

"Thou graspest but half the truth," Rusticus replied, tapping the table with a dull thud, as if to drive the lesson deep. "Epictetus teacheth that to strive for what lieth beyond thy mastery is folly. Thy soul alone is thine to govern—all else, be it mules, carts, or the very city of Rome, is but dust in the wind." He waved a hand toward the sprawl of Rome below, its distant hum a murmur through the fig leaves. "What is dust to thee, Marcus?"

The boy frowned, his thoughts a tangled skein, the splinter beneath his finger a small pain to anchor him. "Is it... naught?" he asked, voice uncertain.

Rusticus let forth a snort, a rare fracture in his stone-like visage. "Nay, lad. Dust is all that thou deemest of worth—thy grandfather's coin, thy aunts' whispers, the Senate's clamour. Dust, all of it. Let it choke thee, and thou art no better than that broken mule thou didst lament."

Marcus' jaw tightened, the words a lash upon his spirit. He recalled the mule, its leg shattered beneath a cart's burden, its cry a keen that pierced the Forum's din. Dust had not seemed naught then, but a weight that bore down upon all. Yet he nodded, for Rusticus sought not debate but understanding, and Marcus was ever loath to gainsay.

Thus passed the hours, a dance of words and silences, Rusticus casting forth lines from Epictetus or Zeno like seeds upon barren soil, waiting for Marcus to nurture them into thought. He did not discourse at length; rather, he prodded, letting the boy stumble through his own reason. Once, he bade Marcus stand and recite a passage whilst balancing a cup of water upon his head—"Govern thy trembling, lest thou spill," he had barked when the water splashed upon the earth. Marcus misliked the task, yet he held his tongue, as was his custom.

Days stretched into weeks, the Palatine's ascent growing less a trial with each dawn, Rusticus' garden a proving ground not of steel but of the mind's mettle. One morn, Marcus arrived ere the sun had fully crested the rooftops, the sky yet tinged with the roseate hues of dawn. Rusticus was pruning a vine, his knife flashing swift as a gladius in a soldier's hand. He offered no greeting, merely pointed to a scroll upon the table, its edges worn as if handled by generations.

"Musonius Rufus," Rusticus declared, his voice a low rumble. "On the virtue of endurance."

Marcus unrolled the scroll, its weight a burden in his hands, the words heavier than Epictetus' had been. Rufus spake of nights chill and cheerless, of bellies empty and bodies broken, yet the spirit unyielding as the oak 'gainst the tempest. He finished, the papyrus damp beneath his fingers, the ink blurring where his sweat had fallen.

Rusticus continued his pruning, the knife's snip-snip a rhythm to his words. "What is endurance to thee, lad?"

Marcus' thoughts turned to his mother, Domitia Lucilla, her gentle tones belying a will that bent not even in widowhood's shadow. He recalled his grandfather, Annius Verus, whose coughs brought forth blood yet signed his decrees with a steady hand. "It is to remain unbroken when affliction presseth sore," he answered, voice soft but firm.

Rusticus paused, the knife hovering o'er a vine, its edge gleaming in the dawn's light. "Near enough," he said, his tone a grudging assent. "Endurance is to choose not to break, though affliction be a guest within thy house. Bid it not linger overlong." He severed the vine with a flick, casting it to the earth. "Inscribe that upon thy tablet."

Marcus scratched the words with his stylus, the wax yielding reluctantly, his hand unsteady. *Affliction is a guest—bid it not linger.* The phrase lodged within his mind, a pebble in a sandal, discomfiting yet persistent. That night, sleep eluded him, the grand house upon the Caelian Hill—his grandfather's, with its polished stone and frescoed walls—too vast, too silent. By the flicker of an oil lamp, its flame spitting and guttering, he wrote upon his tablet, not the words of Rufus, but his own: *The mind may render dust into stone, should it so will.* The line was rough-hewn, yet it was his own, a fledgling thought taking wing.

Weeks hence, a messenger came, breathless and urgent, as Marcus and Rusticus debated in the garden—whether a man might govern his temper, Rusticus asserting aye, Marcus doubting the ease of such mastery. The slave burst through the gate, his tunic stained with sweat, a sealed tablet thrust forth. "From the emperor," he gasped, his breath a ragged plea.

Rusticus raised a brow but spake naught, his pruning knife still in hand. Marcus broke the wax, his heart a drum within his breast, Hadrian's script a spider's crawl upon the tablet: *To Marcus Aurelius Verus, greetings. The Caesar summons thee to the Palatine. Antoninus Pius shall see thee raised.* The year was 138 CE, and the world tilted upon its axis, a new burden descending.

He looked to Rusticus, the tablet trembling in his grasp. "He adopteth me—Antoninus. I am to be—" His voice faltered, the weight of destiny a yoke upon his shoulders.

"Dust," Rusticus interjected, his voice dry as the Palatine's soil. "Titles, marble, crowns—all dust." He stood, brushing the earth from his hands, his gaze piercing as a legionary's spear. "What lieth herein"—he tapped his temple, the gesture sharp—"that alone is thine own. Let not Rome wrest it from thee."

Marcus nodded, though the burden settled heavy, Rome and its throne a mantle he had not sought. He departed the garden, Epictetus' scroll clasped beneath his arm, the city below a beast stirring to devour him whole. Rusticus watched him go, the pruning knife gleaming, and Marcus pondered if he might ever return. Years hence, as emperor upon the Danube's frontier, he would scribe by lamplight in a soldier's tent, the echoes of a boy's words returning: *The mind may render dust into stone.* But such days were yet distant. Now, he was but a youth, sandals worn, descending the Palatine with a tablet scratched full of lessons, and a mind brimming with queries Rusticus had not answered—for perchance, even he knew not how.

THE STOIC EMPEROR

180 AD, DANUBE RIVER (MODERN- DAY AUSTRIA)

Section I: Prologue

arcus Aurelius, the emperor and philosopher-king of Rome, sat alone in his campaign tent, eyes locked on the sagging gray sky that seemed to press down on the northern frontier like a mourner's veil. Beyond the canvas, the wind keened, carrying the sharp tang of scorched earth and pine—a bleak hymn from a land his legions had clawed to keep.

His body rebelled against him, joints grinding, muscles frail beneath the weight of sickness, yet his mind stood apart, a fortress unbreached. This, he knew, was his final march, the last time he'd face the Germanic tribes gnashing at Rome's borders. The thought settled in him, heavy but not unwelcome.

Fever crept through him, a slow tide that left him pallid and trembling, yet he greeted it with the stillness he'd cultivated through decades of discipline. Death hovered near, its breath cold on his neck, but what of it? He'd long ceased to see it as an enemy. It was merely the next turn in the road, as natural as the seasons he'd watched fade and return. Fear, he'd decided years ago, was a choice—and a useless one.

He closed his eyes, letting the rhythm of his breath anchor him, and recalled the words he'd scratched into his meditations: *"Don't act as if you'll live ten thousand years. Death hangs over you. While you live, while you can, be good."* The lines had been his companion through nights like this, a mirror to his soul.

But the empire wouldn't pause for his musings. Its edges frayed under the tribes' ceaseless raids, peace a fragile thing stitched with blood and bartered promises. His generals were already mapping the next strike, their voices faint beyond the tent's walls. The weight of Rome—of millions who looked to him—pressed against his chest, as real as the winter chill seeping through the canvas. To rule was to carry this load, to stand firm even as his own frame buckled. He didn't resent it. He couldn't. Resentment would mean denying what was.

A gust shook the tent, tugging him from his reverie. He opened his eyes, peering toward the flap where shadows moved—armor glinting, voices murmuring, fires spitting against the dark. His army churned out there, a living machine unaware of the quiet war their emperor waged within. Soldiers sharpened swords, the scrape of stone on steel a steady pulse in the night. Men crouched by flames, hands outstretched to fend off the cold, their whispers threading through the air— some taut with dread, others soft with pleas to gods who might not hear. Marcus watched them, his gaze lingering on faces still bright with youth, unscarred by the truths he'd come to know.

What was life, he wondered, but this fleeting flare against the void? These men brimmed with it—vigor, hope, the raw will to fight—while he felt it slipping from his grasp. He'd seen too much to trust its permanence: Parthian blades flashing in the east, barbarian hordes crashing like waves in the north, the Antonine Plague carving its slow, merciless path through Rome. The empire had reeled, and he'd borne its pain as his own, a mantle he'd never sought but never shirked. How many times had he stood here, on the edge of another battle, knowing lives would spill under his command? Too many to count, too few to forget.

Did it matter? The question gnawed at him, insistent. He'd ruled as a philosopher, wielding power with reason's steady hand, striving to shield Rome from its own rot and the enemies at its gates. Yet what was one man's reign against the sweep of time? Would his name echo, or crumble like the statues of forgotten kings?

He turned the thought over, examining it as he would a stone in his palm. Perhaps it didn't matter—not in the way men craved. He'd written it himself: *"You have power over your mind, not the chaos beyond. Grasp this, and you'll find peace."* The empire's fate, the whims of history—those were currents he couldn't steer. His task was simpler, sharper: to meet this moment, and the next, as himself.

The sickness tightened its hold, a dull ache threading through his bones. It whispered of time's limits, but he refused to let it drown his thoughts. Duty endured, a tether pulling him forward—one last campaign, one final act for Rome. He shifted in his chair, spine straightening against the protest of his body. Emperor or not, dying or not, he remained the man who chose to stand.

He rose, joints flaring with pain he dismissed like a fleeting thought. Draping his cloak over his shoulders, he stepped into the wind's bite. The camp hushed as he emerged, soldiers pausing mid-task, eyes lifting to him. They stood straighter, hands stilled, a reverence rippling through the ranks. "Caesar," they murmured, salutes sharp against the dusk. He nodded, moving among them with measured steps, pausing to ask after their readiness, their lives—quiet words that tied him to them, not as a distant ruler but as a man they'd bled beside.

They saw past the gaunt face, the hollowed frame. In his eyes burned the fire of the Stoic who'd led them through shadow after shadow, who faced ruin with a calm they couldn't fathom. They'd march for him, into whatever waited beyond the horizon, because he'd walked the path first.

Back in his tent, the cold burrowed deep, his body quaking faintly from the effort. His mind, though, held clear as dawn. Battles had marked his years—on fields, in councils, within the chambers of his own soul. Now, one more loomed, the last.

And he was ready.

Section II: The Call of Duty

In the faint glow of the war council tent, Marcus Aurelius occupied the head of a broad oak table, encircled by his most loyal commanders. Scattered across the tabletop were maps and parchments, tracing the recent maneuvers of the Germanic tribes probing the empire's edges. The tent's atmosphere thickened with fervent debate, as his officers clashed over strategies, their voices climbing in a tangle of urgency. Some pressed for a rapid counterstrike, eager to punish the invaders, while others urged restraint, their caution born of bitter losses on unfamiliar ground.

Marcus lingered in silence, hands resting lightly on his chair's arms, his presence a still point amid the storm. His gaze drifted across the maps, unfocused, the lines and symbols blurring as his thoughts turned inward. Countless battles and campaigns had woven war into the fabric of his existence, a relentless tide he'd learned to navigate. Yet it wasn't the tribal threats or the perils of combat that gripped him now—it was something closer, something heavier.

His mind settled on the figure beside him: his son, Commodus, the uncertain heir to all he'd built.

Commodus sat to his right, restless, fingers toying with his sword's pommel, his posture shifting with barely contained impatience. His eyes roamed the tent, flitting over the generals, detached from the grave matters unfolding before him. Marcus sensed the unease pouring off his son, a young man whose thoughts strayed far from the council's weighty discourse, far from the mantle of leadership that loomed ever nearer. It gnawed at him, a quiet ache beneath his ribs. The empire's frontiers teetered on the brink, but the destiny of Rome itself— the legacy of centuries—pressed heavier still, a burden he could not shake.

He observed Commodus quietly, tracing the youthful cast of his features, the hunger for acclaim glinting in his eyes, the unchecked ambition Marcus had never managed to bridle. This had always been his fear, a shadow that grew with each passing year. His son, heir to the mightiest realm on earth, showed scant regard for the Stoic principles—discipline, reason—that had steered Marcus through the chaos of his reign. Commodus was a different breed: rash, captivated by grandeur and indulgence, a flame flickering too wild to be tamed. The emperor had striven to mold him, to impart the virtues of a sage ruler through patient lessons and hard-won example, but here, in this pivotal hour, it was plain: Commodus was unready, and perhaps always would be.

The generals' voices swelled, a rising tide that tugged Marcus back to the moment. He blinked, refocusing on the table, the maps snapping into clarity once more. He couldn't let his dread over Commodus cloud his duty—not now, not with Rome's fate hanging in the balance. The empire faced war once more, its borders tested by relentless foes, and the legions looked to him for guidance. With a measured breath, he steadied himself, preparing to speak, though the shadow of the future lingered in his chest, a weight no armor could deflect.

The debate grew fiercer, each officer more adamant than the last, their words clashing like swords. "We must hit them before winter locks us in," a grizzled commander insisted, stabbing a finger at the map, his voice rough with conviction. "They're fractured now, ripe for the taking. A bold push will shatter them before they rally."

Another leaned in, brow creased with dissent, his tone sharp. "And then what? Charging in blind could leave us stranded in hostile lands. The tribes are sly—they'll lure us into ruin if we leap too soon."

Marcus held his tongue, absorbing the rising clamor, his silence a counterpoint to their urgency. The room pulsed with impatience; even these battle-worn men ached for an end to the endless strife, their spirits frayed by years of conflict. Then Commodus broke in, his voice slicing through the din with brash confidence, a young lion eager to roar. "Why dither?" he declared, leaning forward, eyes alight with zeal. "Smash them hard and fast—we'll crush them. The quicker we finish this, the sooner we haul back the spoils and the fame."

Heads swiveled toward him, reactions ranging from curiosity to wariness, a ripple of tension spreading through the tent. Marcus felt a familiar knot tighten within, a blend of exasperation and unease that had grown all too common. His son's lust for glory was as perilous as it was green, a spark that could ignite disaster.

"Glory isn't war's purpose, Commodus," Marcus replied, his tone even but resolute, cutting through the air like a honed blade. He knew the pull of battle's thrill, the itch to charge ahead for renown—he'd felt it once, long ago. Yet war, he'd learned through blood and years, wasn't about personal laurels—it was about endurance, foresight, and restraint, virtues his son had yet to grasp.

Commodus' expression dimmed, though defiance lingered in the set of his jaw. "But Father, stalling only strengthens them. We should strike while they're frail."

Marcus inhaled deeply, his gaze sweeping the table of weathered generals, each face etched with the scars of past campaigns. "What you see as frailty is their lure," he said steadily, his voice a calm anchor in the storm. "Rush in without care, and we dance to their tune. Overreach, and our legions falter—they thrive in this harshness; we do not."

Doubtful looks flickered among the officers, their eyes tracing his thinning frame, the lines of sickness etched into his face. They revered Marcus, their emperor and warlord, yet his frailty was undeniable, and to some, his prudence smacked of an old man's caution, a hesitance born of waning strength.

A younger general, keen to prove himself, spoke up, his voice edged with impatience. "Caesar, with respect, this war's dragged on too long. The troops chafe. Delay more, and we lose the drive to break them for good."

Marcus turned his weary eyes to the man, unflinching, his gaze steady despite the exhaustion pulling at him. He grasped their restiveness, their thirst for a decisive blow—he'd felt it too, in younger days. But he also knew the worth of wisdom over haste, a truth carved from decades of command, from victories won not by might but by mind. "Don't confuse caution with frailty," he said softly, though his voice carried authority, a quiet force that stilled the room. "We've triumphed before—not by lunging blindly, but by biding our time, plotting each step. You chase this fight; I guard Rome's endurance."

Silence fell, his words sinking in, a heavy truth settling over the council. Marcus felt their unspoken doubts—about his vigor, his grip on power—but his stare held firm, unyielding as the marble of Rome's foundations. He'd led them through darker trials than this, through plagues and rebellions, and he would again. "Recall the Quadi," he pressed, invoking a past triumph, his voice steady with memory. "We prevailed not by raw might, but by waiting, by reading their moves before we struck. This is no different."

He glanced at Commodus, now quiet, the boy's earlier bravado muted, then back to the council, his resolve unshaken. "We'll act—but not rashly. Dispatch scouts. Gauge their numbers, their ground. When the hour ripens, we move." For a beat, no one stirred, the weight of his command hanging in the air. Then, slowly, the generals nodded, bowing to his seasoned judgment, their trust in him overriding their doubts. Though age and ailment had worn his body, Marcus' mind remained a honed blade, and they'd heed him, as ever.

Commodus shifted, his face taut with suppressed irritation, the unquenched yearning for glory simmering beneath his silence. Marcus saw it, felt it, the restless fire that refused to be banked, but the matter was settled—for now.

The council dispersed, the tent's tension hanging like stale smoke, a lingering echo of clashing wills. Marcus stayed seated as the generals departed, his gaze tracking Commodus, who rose with restless vigor, a caged beast eager to prowl. Sensing a need for words unspoken, Marcus gestured for his son to remain, the air between them thick with what was left unsaid.

Alone now, he spoke, his voice low yet firm, laden with a father's care and an emperor's duty, each word weighted by years of struggle. "Commodus, I must speak plainly." His son halted, arms folded, impatience plain in the tilt of his head, the tightness of his stance. Marcus steadied himself against the ache gnawing his frame, a dull fire that never ceased. "This path you crave—swift glory, instant wins—it's treacherous," he began, eyes locked on his son, searching for a spark of understanding. "Unreined ambition is a blaze that devours its wielder and all he touches. Rome has endured centuries not by recklessness, but by order, patience, and tempered strength."

Commodus shifted, his look mingling annoyance with apathy, a wall rising between them. "Father, I only—" Marcus lifted a hand, cutting him off, his gesture sharp but weary.

"I know your intent, Commodus. You yearn to carve your name in triumph, to seize the laurels of victory with your own hands. But true victory isn't a fleeting clash—it's safeguarding something vaster than us: the empire. A leader must see past the fray, past his own desires, to the horizon beyond." His words flowed steady but worn, drawn from a lifetime's hard-earned insight, a wellspring deep and bittersweet.

"You need restraint, Commodus. To act blind to the fallout is to steer Rome toward collapse. That's not the heritage I seek to pass on, nor one I wish for you." He saw the flicker of indignation in his son's eyes, the restless shifting of his frame. Commodus stood rigid, gaze drifting as if already elsewhere, lost to the arena's roar, the promise of easy victories. Marcus had tried, time and again, to instill the values that upheld Rome—patience, discipline, the quiet strength of reason—but now, facing his son, he saw those seeds hadn't sprouted, their roots too shallow to hold.

The emperor exhaled slowly, the weight of his sickness pressing anew, a tide of fatigue that threatened to pull him under. His once-robust frame quaked with exhaustion, a shadow of the warrior he'd been, yet his will endured. He could only hope time might yet teach Commodus what he wouldn't hear now, that the years might temper what words could not.

"Ponder my words," Marcus finished, his tone gentling, a father's plea beneath the emperor's command. "Rome's fate will soon be yours to bear. Mind that charge."

Commodus offered a curt nod, half-hearted, his indifference clear in the slump of his shoulders, the distance in his eyes. Marcus knew his counsel hadn't pierced the young man's armor of ambition, hadn't breached the walls of his restless heart. A quiet grief tugged at him, sharp and deep, his time to shape his son slipping through his fingers like sand.

Worn by illness and unheard wisdom, Marcus rose, legs unsteady but pride unbowed, refusing to let his frailty show more than it must. Commodus lingered briefly, then strode out, unchanged, his steps quick and careless.

Alone, Marcus stood in the tent's stillness, the empire's uncertain horizon looming large, a vast and shadowed expanse. His son wasn't prepared—might never be—and that fear outstripped any foe beyond the borders, a wound no strategy could heal. The tribes could be felled, their spears broken by Roman steel, but Rome's succession was a fight beyond his sword, a battle waged in silence and doubt. With a heavy sigh, he stepped into the chill night, the cold biting at his bones.

The stars gleamed above, heedless of mortal cares, as they had for ages, their light a distant, unchanging witness. Marcus gazed upward, the burden of his reign a yoke on his shoulders, pressing down with every step. He'd guided Rome through wars, plagues, and turmoil, his hands steady on the reins through every storm, but now, as his days dwindled, the empire's tomorrow hung in doubt, a thread fraying in the wind. Yet he recalled the Stoic creed that had long sustained him, a quiet mantra against the dark: *You can't sway what comes. Only how you meet it.*

With that, Marcus Aurelius turned toward his quarters, bearing the load of an uncharted future with the quiet resolve that had defined him always.

Section III: March to the Danube

The Roman army set out at dawn, the first light of the sun breaking through the overcast sky, casting a pale glow over the landscape. The long line of soldiers stretched far into the distance, their armor glinting faintly in the dim light as they began their march northward toward the Danube. The sound of thousands of feet moving in unison filled the cold air, a steady, rhythmic drumbeat that echoed through the dense forest surrounding them.

At the head of the column, where Marcus Aurelius once would have ridden on horseback, a covered carriage now moved at a slow, deliberate pace. Inside, the emperor sat wrapped in furs, his body too frail to endure the rigors of riding. His illness had worsened, and each passing day drained more of his strength. The fever came and went, leaving him in a perpetual state of fatigue, but his mind, sharpened by years of Stoic discipline, remained as clear as the winter air outside.

Through the small opening of the carriage, Marcus watched his legions march. The soldiers moved with practiced precision, their faces set with determination, their breath visible in the morning chill. They were hardened men, veterans of long campaigns, and yet, as Marcus gazed upon them, he saw more than just soldiers. He saw the weight of the empire they carried with them—the burden of protecting Rome, of defending its borders from the relentless waves of barbarian incursions.

His thoughts drifted back to earlier campaigns, when he had led the charge on horseback, his body strong and unyielding. He remembered the thrill of battle, the way his presence had inspired his men. But those days were gone now. His body had become a cage, weakened and worn, yet his spirit remained intact. He knew that this campaign might be his last, but even so, he was determined to see it through. Rome needed him, now more than ever.

The soldiers passed through the forest, the towering trees casting long shadows over the road. The forest was quiet, save for the steady clanking of armor and the crunch of boots on frozen ground. Marcus watched it all with the calm detachment of a philosopher, observing without judgment. He could not control the external world; the outcome of the battle, the weather, the illness that ravaged his body, but he could control his mind, his reaction to it all.

The Stoic lessons he had carried with him throughout his life whispered in his thoughts: *"The impediment to action advances action. What stands in the way becomes the way."* His sickness was merely another obstacle, another test. He would endure it, as he had endured all things, with patience and acceptance.

As the army passed through the remnants of villages that had once thrived along the northern frontier, the scars of war were everywhere. Broken walls and charred beams jutted from the earth, the skeletons of homes that had been reduced to ruin in earlier skirmishes with the Germanic tribes. The land itself seemed tired, worn down by the constant cycle of conflict that had consumed it for decades. The soldiers moved in silence, their eyes forward, but the weight of their surroundings pressed heavily on them.

From his carriage, Marcus Aurelius watched it all, his thoughts heavy with reflection. The soldiers who marched before him were young, many barely older than boys. Their faces, hardened by battle yet still full of zeal, reminded him of the legions he had once led, of the warriors who had followed him into countless battles. They moved with purpose, driven by the desire to protect their empire, to serve something greater than themselves. But as Marcus gazed at their youthful faces, he couldn't help but wonder if they truly understood the price of victory.

War, he knew, was not the grand spectacle that many of them believed it to be. It was not the stories of heroism and glory that were told in the barracks or whispered around campfires. War was brutal, unforgiving, and ultimately, transient. The battles won today would fade into memory, just as the ruins of these villages were now fading into the landscape. The young soldiers who marched with such determination would soon bear the scars of battle, both on their bodies and in their souls. Many would not return home.

In the stillness of his carriage, Marcus leaned back against the worn cushions, his breath slow and steady despite the cold that seeped through the fabric. He closed his eyes for a moment, turning his thoughts inward, drawing on the Stoic philosophy that had guided him through years of war and hardship.

"War is merely another part of nature's order," he mused to himself, the words forming clearly in his mind. *"A conflict of forces, a natural consequence of men and nations seeking survival, dominance, or peace. Just as life and death are part of the cycle, so too is war. It is neither to be celebrated nor condemned-merely accepted."*

He opened his eyes again, his gaze returning to the soldiers trudging through the snow. They did not yet understand that war, like life itself, was impermanent. They fought for victory, for the promise of peace, but peace was always fleeting. Another enemy would rise, another battle would come, and the cycle would begin anew. Marcus had come to accept this long ago. His role as emperor was to guide his people through these inevitable struggles, to protect Rome as best he could, even if it meant marching into battle once again.

The wind howled, shaking the trees and stirring the snow in swirling gusts. Marcus wrapped his cloak tighter around his frail frame, feeling the cold deep in his bones.

The soldiers' faces blurred into the landscape as the army continued its slow, steady march toward the Danube. And as Marcus gazed out at them, he could not help but think of the countless generations of men who had marched this same path, fought these same battles, only to be forgotten by history.

"We are but a brief moment in the vastness of time," he reflected. *"Yet in that moment, we must act with purpose, with reason, with virtue."*

The journey was hard, but Marcus knew that his purpose, and that of his legions, would endure. The march would continue, as would the war. And so, too, would life.

Section IV: The Battle

The armies of Rome and the Germanic tribes faced each other across a vast, frozen plain, the air thick with the tension of impending violence. The earth beneath the soldiers' feet was hard as stone, covered in a thin sheet of snow that crunched with every movement. On one side, the Roman legions stood in disciplined formation, their armor gleaming despite the biting cold, shields locked together in preparation for the advance. Across from them, the Germanic tribes gathered in loose ranks, their warriors wild and fierce, clad in furs and leathers, their breath visible in the frigid air as they shouted war cries to the heavens.

From a hill overlooking the battlefield, Marcus Aurelius watched it all unfold, his heart heavy with the weight of leadership. Too ill to join his men in the thick of the fight, he stood draped in a thick cloak, his frail form almost lost against the harsh landscape. His face was pale, his body weakened by the sickness that had plagued him for months, yet his presence was steady, his mind sharp and focused. His generals gathered around him, awaiting his final commands before the clash began.

Marcus gazed down at the field below, his eyes moving from the disciplined ranks of his soldiers to the chaotic mass of the enemy. This battle, like so many before it, would be brutal. He knew the cost would be great; the bodies of men would litter the snow before the sun set, their blood staining the frozen earth. But Rome had no choice. The Germanic tribes threatened the empire's borders, and peace, if it could be won, would only come through decisive action.

With a slow, deliberate breath, Marcus turned to his generals. His voice, though quiet, carried a calm authority that belied his physical weakness. "The time has come," he said, his words measured and clear. "Our legions will advance in formation. No one breaks ranks, no matter the provocation. Hold the line."

The generals nodded, their faces grave.

"The cavalry will circle to the north," Marcus continued, pointing to a distant rise that overlooked the enemy's flank. "We will strike them from two sides. This battle will not be won with brute force alone. Precision and discipline will carry the day."

One by one, the generals saluted and left to deliver the emperor's orders to their men. Marcus remained on the hill, watching the lines of Roman soldiers shift into position. The cold wind tugged at his cloak, biting at his skin, but he stood firm. His eyes narrowed as he looked across the plain at the distant figures of the Germanic warriors, shouting and banging their weapons against their shields. They were fierce, unyielding, driven by desperation and fury. They would not go down easily.

When the signal was given, a horn blaring across the icy expanse, the Roman legions began their advance. Shields raised, spears bristling, they moved as one- an impenetrable wall of steel and discipline. Marcus watched them go, his heart heavy with the knowledge of what was to come. He had seen it too many times before; the chaos, the screams, the carnage of war. No matter how carefully they planned, no matter how disciplined his legions, the cost would always be paid in blood.

His breath misted in the cold air as the first clash of metal echoed across the plain. The battle had begun, and Rome's fate, once again, hung in the balance.

The battlefield erupted into chaos as soon as the two forces met, the clash of shields and swords reverberating through the frozen air. The Roman legions held their disciplined formations, their shields locked tight as they pushed against the wild, furious charges of the Germanic warriors. The sound of steel striking steel rang out like thunder, mingled with the shouts of commanders and the guttural cries of men locked in deadly combat. The snow beneath their feet quickly turned red as bodies fell, both Roman and barbarian alike, claimed by the relentless violence of war.

From his vantage point on the hill, Marcus Aurelius watched the carnage unfold, his face an unreadable mask of stoic calm. His generals stood nearby, awaiting his orders, but Marcus gave them sparingly, only speaking when the tide of battle required a shift in strategy. His mind, ever calculating, analyzed the movements of the enemy, anticipating their next attacks, ensuring that his legions held the line where it mattered most. And yet, beneath the cold logic of military command, his thoughts wandered to deeper, darker places.

The brutality unfolding before him was all too familiar. He had witnessed it countless times in his life; battle after battle, year after year, men dying by the hundreds, their lives extinguished in a matter of moments. And for what? A stretch of land? The fragile concept of power? Victory, Marcus knew, was always fleeting. It was earned with blood, only to be challenged again by the next wave of enemies or the next ambition of men. The glory of conquest was an illusion, and war, for all its necessity, was nothing more than a cycle of destruction.

He allowed his mind to drift further, his eyes still fixed on the field but his thoughts somewhere beyond it. The Stoic teachings he had adhered to for so long whispered to him now, offering perspective in the midst of chaos. *"What is evil? It is the war you wage within yourself."* He had written those words once, long ago, when reflecting on the internal struggles that each man must face. War was not only fought on the battlefield; the true battle lay within–against pride, against anger, against the illusion of control.

Marcus knew that external conflicts–these wars with barbarians, the defense of Rome's borders–were a part of the natural order of human affairs. But he had come to understand that they were not the true battles. The real struggle, the one that mattered, was the one each man waged against his own nature. To be consumed by hatred, by vengeance, by the need for dominance- these were the true enemies. And as he watched the battlefield below, he couldn't help but see the futility of it all.

The Germanic tribes fought with a fury born of desperation, and his legions, disciplined and unyielding, fought with the grim determination to protect what they had sworn to defend. But in the end, it was the same. Men killing men, nations clashing for power, only for another war to follow in the years to come. It was a cycle that had existed long before him and would continue long after he was gone. And yet, as emperor, he was bound to it. He had a duty to protect Rome, to lead his people through these wars, no matter how senseless they seemed to his philosopher's mind.

Another wave of barbarians surged forward, and Marcus gave a brief order to one of his generals to reinforce the left flank. His voice was calm, steady, despite the chaos below. He had learned long ago to detach himself from the emotions of the moment, to observe the battle with the same clarity he brought to all things. But inwardly, he could not help but reflect on the nature of war, and the irony that it was the same virtues, discipline, patience, and control, that enabled him to command armies while also revealing to him the ultimate futility of their efforts.

"War is merely another form of nature," he reminded himself, *"no different from the storm or the flood. It destroys, but it also clears the way for something new."* Yet, in this moment, as he watched men fall to the ground, their lives snuffed out in an instant, Marcus could not help but feel the weight of it all.

The battle raged on, and Marcus continued to lead, issuing orders with the precision of a seasoned general. But in his heart, he knew the truth: Rome's survival depended on these victories but victory itself was a transient thing. It was a brief respite in the endless conflict of the world, just as life was a brief flicker in the vastness of time.

And as the wind howled across the battlefield, carrying the screams and cries of the dying, Marcus Aurelius stood on the hill, his thoughts far beyond the clashing of swords, focused instead on the eternal struggle that raged within the hearts of men.

The tide of battle slowly shifted in Rome's favor. The disciplined Roman legions, bolstered by strategic maneuvers and unyielding formations, began to push the Germanic tribes back across the frozen plain. The barbarians fought fiercely, driven by desperation, but the relentless pressure of the Roman advance proved too much. One by one, the enemy lines began to break. Men who had charged forward with wild fury now stumbled back, slipping in the blood-soaked snow as they retreated in disarray.

From his vantage point on the hill, Marcus Aurelius watched it all unfold. He could see the barbarians falling back, their once-thundering war cries reduced to scattered shouts of panic as their formation crumbled. The Roman soldiers, sensing the shift, pressed harder, their shields pushing the enemy back with each coordinated step. The battle was nearing its end, the outcome now clear to all who fought on that desolate field.

The cheers of the Roman soldiers rose in the cold air, a sound of triumph and relief after hours of brutal combat. The victory was theirs. The Germanic tribes were retreating, their strength broken, their warriors scattered. But as Marcus stood there, gazing out over the battlefield, he felt no surge of pride, no satisfaction in the victory that his legions had achieved.

Instead, his heart was heavy with the cost of it all. The plain below him was littered with bodies–Romans and barbarians alike–men who had fought and died for a cause, for a piece of land, for the idea of victory. The snow had been stained red with their blood, and the sight of it filled Marcus not with triumph, but with sorrow. He had seen this before, so many times, and he knew he would see it again.

The cheers of the soldiers grew louder as the last of the barbarians fled, but Marcus remained silent, his gaze distant. He had won the battle, yes–but at what cost? How many lives had been sacrificed for this fleeting moment of peace? How many fathers, brothers, and sons lay dead on that frozen field, their lives cut short by the endless march of war?

He turned slowly from the battlefield, his body trembling from both the cold and the illness that gnawed at his strength. The generals gathered around him, offering their congratulations, but Marcus waved them away with a gentle motion.

As he looked over his legions, who now cheered in the glow of their hard-won triumph, Marcus understood better than anyone that this was not the end. Peace, if it could even be called that, would not last. Another war would come, another battle would be fought, and the cycle would continue. It always did.

The soldiers could not see what he saw. To them, this victory was a triumph, a moment to celebrate. But to Marcus, it was merely a brief respite in the endless struggle for power, for survival. The empire might have been secured for another day, but the forces that threatened it, from within and outside, would never be fully defeated.

"Peace is never permanent," Marcus thought to himself, the words heavy in his mind. *"Victory is but a fleeting thing."*

As the echoes of celebration carried across the battlefield, Marcus quietly turned away, his cloak pulled tight against the biting wind. He walked slowly back toward his camp, leaving the battlefield behind, knowing that his work was far from finished. There would always be another battle, another struggle to face. But for now, he would rest and prepare for whatever came next.

The cheers of the soldiers faded into the distance as Marcus disappeared into the cold, his thoughts already far from the battlefield. He had won the day, but the war, in all its forms, would never truly end.

Section V: Nightfall

In the quiet of his tent, Marcus Aurelius sat alone, the faint flicker of an oil lamp casting long shadows that danced along the walls. The cold had seeped into his bones, a persistent chill that no amount of furs could entirely ward off. His breathing was labored now, each breath a struggle, as if his body was already preparing to surrender to the inevitable. He could feel it–death, not as an ominous threat, but as a companion, drawing closer with each passing day.

Before him on a small wooden table lay his journal, the leather-bound pages worn from years of use. His hand, though trembling slightly, moved steadily across the parchment, the words flowing as if they were his final conversation with himself. He had always turned to his writings in moments of quiet reflection, using them to capture his thoughts, to remind himself of the principles that had guided his life. Tonight was no different, except that now he wrote with the clear understanding that these words would likely be his last.

He paused for a moment, the quill hovering over the page, as he considered the thought forming in his mind. There was no fear, no regret; only the calm acceptance of what was to come. He dipped the quill in ink again and continued, his handwriting deliberate and slow.

"It is not death that a man should fear, but never beginning to live."

He allowed the words to settle on the page before him, nodding slightly to himself. Death had never been something he feared. He had lived with the knowledge of its approach for as long as he could remember, and now, as he faced it head-on, he felt only a quiet resignation. Life, he knew, was fleeting, a brief flicker in the vast expanse of time, and to live in fear of death was to waste the very thing that made life precious. What mattered was not how long one lived, but how one lived, the choices made, the principles upheld.

The lamp flickered, casting a brief shadow over the page, but Marcus kept writing. He wrote about life, about duty, about the endless cycles of nature and the universe. He wrote about the Stoic virtues that had sustained him—patience, temperance, wisdom—and how these virtues had allowed him to lead not just as an emperor, but as a man. In these final reflections, there was no lament, no bitterness. Only clarity.

Outside the tent, the camp was quiet, the soldiers resting after the brutal battle fought earlier that day. But inside, Marcus was awake, alone with his thoughts, preparing for the final journey that all men must one day take.

Death was not the enemy. It was simply the end of a life lived with purpose, and Marcus Aurelius, as he sat by the dim glow of the oil lamp, knew that his time had come. The cold that gripped him was no longer a thing to fight against, but something to accept, as natural as the passing of seasons. He had lived, he had ruled, and now, he was ready for what came next.

Marcus paused in his writing, his hand hovering over the parchment as the weight of his reflections settled on him. His gaze drifted from the flickering flame of the oil lamp to the shadows on the tent's walls, his mind wandering back through the years of his life. He had lived a life few men could imagine—an emperor, a philosopher, a warrior. His reign had been marked by endless trials: wars, plagues, political unrest. Yet through it all, he had strived to rule with reason, justice, and the virtues that had shaped him.

But as his thoughts traveled the long roads of his past, they inevitably turned toward the future, and to the one uncertainty that troubled him most: Commodus. His son. The heir to all that Marcus had built. The young man who would soon inherit the empire but lacked the wisdom, the discipline, and the virtue to rule it.

Marcus had tried, again and again, to instill in Commodus the values that had sustained him, the principles of Stoicism that guided his life. He had counseled patience, reason, and the need to rise above base desires, but Commodus had always been a different kind of man. Restless, ambitious, driven by impulses that Marcus had never fully understood. The weight of the empire's legacy, which had pressed so heavily on Marcus' own shoulders, seemed lost on his son.

Can Rome survive under his rule? The question gnawed at Marcus, though he knew it was one to which he had no answer. He could not change his son, just as he could not change the course of his own fate. Commodus would inherit the empire, and with it, the responsibilities Marcus had borne for decades. But what Commodus would make of it, Marcus could not control. And that, more than anything, filled him with quiet sorrow.

But what is power, truly? he mused, his hand trembling as he wrote. *To seek control over that which is uncontrollable is folly.* Marcus had always known this. The Stoic teachings reminded him time and again: one cannot control the actions of others, only one's own responses to the world. He could not change Commodus, nor could he alter the future. All that was left for him to do was to accept the inevitable with grace, just as he had accepted the battles, the losses, the victories, and now, his own death.

His writing slowed further, the words faltering as his hand grew heavier. The flickering light of the oil lamp seemed to grow dimmer, and the cold in his bones deepened. He had faced so much in his life, but this, his son's unpreparedness for the immense burden ahead, was the one thing that truly weighed on him in these final moments.

Marcus laid down the quill for a moment, resting his hand on the worn surface of the table. He closed his eyes, allowing the silence of the night to wash over him. He could feel the pull of sleep, of something deeper, drawing him closer. He had done all he could. His reign was ending, and soon, the future of Rome would no longer be in his hands.

And so, with the same calm acceptance that had guided him through life, Marcus breathed deeply and reached for the quill once more, determined to finish the final words of his last entry.

Marcus set down his pen, his hand resting on the final words he had written. His breath came slower now, each rise and fall of his chest more labored than the last, yet there was a stillness within him. The flickering light of the oil lamp illuminated the pages of his journal, the ink still fresh. His eyes lingered on the passage, the words echoing back to him with quiet certainty:

"You have lived as a citizen in a great city; five years or a hundred—what does it matter? The laws of that city are the same. And what does nature demand? That you depart with grace, as you entered with grace."

The reflection was clear, its truth resonating through his thoughts. He had lived his life not seeking to avoid death, but to approach it with the same dignity with which he had lived. In those final moments, the teachings that had guided him through war, plague, and the relentless burden of leadership now guided him to his end. Death was not an enemy to be fought but a natural passage, one he had long prepared for.

"Do not act as if you had ten thousand years to live. Death hangs over you. While you live, while it is in your power, be good."

He had written these words to himself in earlier years, a reminder that life's value was not in its length but in how it was lived. Now, as his time drew near, he understood this with perfect clarity. He had ruled with justice, served his people, and strived to live by the virtues of patience, wisdom, and humility. What more could a man ask for?

The cold night air seeped further into the tent, wrapping itself around him, but Marcus felt a warmth rising within him; an unexpected comfort, born not from his failing body but from the knowledge that he had faced his life and his impending death with grace.

With a deliberate breath, Marcus reflected on one last teaching that had always resonated with him: *"Death, like birth, is one of nature's secrets. We must accept it with serenity, as we accept the change of seasons, the passing of time."* He had long understood that life, like the universe, moved in cycles. His cycle was ending, and he welcomed it, knowing that it was but a part of the greater whole.

His hand trembled as he set down the quill, his body weakened by the cold and illness, but his mind remained strong, unwavering in its acceptance. He had made peace with what was to come. Death was not something to be feared, but to be met with calm and dignity, a final duty in the order of things.

Marcus lay back on his cot, the furs wrapped around him offering little protection from the chill of the night. His breathing grew shallower, his chest rising and falling with effort, but his thoughts remained steady. He had done all that could be done. He had lived, ruled, and now, it was time to rest.

The oil lamp beside him flickered, the flame guttering as it struggled against the cold air. He closed his eyes, his thoughts quieting. Soon, his breath slowed, each one softer than the last, until the tent fell silent.

Marcus Aurelius, the philosopher-emperor, passed into history as he had lived: with calm acceptance, his soul carried on the quiet certainty of his Stoic teachings. And in the stillness of that final moment, the man who had ruled the Roman Empire with wisdom and virtue was at peace.

THE BATTLE

BASED ON A TRUE STORY
1097 AD, THE BATTLE OF DORYLAEUM

<u>Bohemond of Taranto</u>

When the sun, a fiery orb scarce risen, clomb the jagged peaks of Phrygia, its wan light cast shadows long and lean upon the earth, as if to etch a dire frontier 'twixt the quick and the dead. Bohemond of Taranto, scion of that fierce Norman sire Robert Guiscard, stood upon the bloodied sward of Dorylaeum, his eyes—azure as the seas that gird Apulia—squinted 'gainst the dawn's harsh glare. The air hung heavy, laden with the fetor of war: sweat, blood, the acrid bite of dread—a miasma that burrowed deep, a grim leech upon the soul, haunting a man long after the clash of steel had faded into memory.

His host, nigh six thousand souls, knelt in a ring about him, shields aloft, a frail rampart 'gainst the ceaseless storm of Seljuk darts that whirred and shrieked from the heavens. Seven hours had they endured this torment—seven hours pinned 'gainst the rugged hills, the mountains a stern warder at their backs, offering no succor, no retreat. Bohemond bore his oaken shield, its weight a growing yoke, yet he held fast. His men—knights of Apulia, Lombardy, Francia—gazed upon him as their lodestar, their prince, their warlord, heir to a lineage of conquest forged in the crucible of Norman ambition. He would not let their faith waver. Yet within his breast stirred a tempest, a gnawing doubt that whispered of the cost of this holy war— a cost he had scarce weighed when he took the cross at Clermont, swayed by dreams of glory as much as piety.

Beside him, a young knight of Rouen, scarce twenty winters, quailed under the sun's cruel fire. His shield drooped, as if the weight of heaven's wrath pressed upon him. Bohemond, iron-willed, struck the lad's ribs with a sharp elbow. "Stir thyself, whelp!" he roared, voice a thunderclap, honed by years of commanding men to slaughter. "Thou fightest for Christ's own glory, not thy craven hide! Let not the Almighty behold thy weakness, lest thou bring shame upon us all!" The knight jolted upright, visage a mask of dread and fervor, a mirror to the countless souls Bohemond had led into the maw of war. Grim. Harsh. War forged men, smelting youth into steel, stripping innocence with each crimson dawn. Bohemond knew its price—too well. Yet he could not turn from it. His name, his ambition, his very blood was bound to the cross he bore, a sacred vow entwined with dreams of a princedom in the East.

A fresh swarm of arrows soared, a dark blight 'gainst the heavens, ere they plunged upon the host with deadly intent. Bohemond braced. Shouts. Groans. The faint keening of women and children amidst the baggage train pierced the din— their sorrow a bitter token of the stakes. Some shafts found flesh, slipping through gaps in the shield-wall. The air was rent with the anguished cries of the stricken—knights, yeomen, their lifeblood seeping into the dust. Priests in tattered vestments lifted voices in fervent supplication, beseeching the Lord for deliverance, their chants a desperate counterpoint to the clamor. Bohemond's hand tightened on his shield, fingers white, thoughts straying to the day this quest was set aflame, a memory sharp as a whetted blade, burning bright.

At Clermont, Pope Urban II had stood afore a mighty throng, lords and knights from Christendom's far corners, his voice a clarion, a spark that set their souls ablaze. He spake of Saracens who defiled the Holy Sepulchre, of pilgrims ravaged by infidel steel, of a Christendom imperiled by the crescent's shadow. "Deus vult!" the host had roared, a tempest that seemed to quake the very earth. "God wills it!" The Pope's gaze had found Bohemond, marking his valor, a courage tempered in the fires of Sicily, Calabria, where he had wrested lands from Greek and Saracen alike. Urban had charged him with this sacred duty—a crusade to reclaim the East, a promise of salvation, yes, but also dominion. Lands. A princedom to rival his father's legacy. How could he refuse? Yet now, kneeling in the mire, the moans of the dying a dirge, Bohemond pondered the true weight of that vow. God's will—or his own ambition, cloaked in piety? A question that gnawed, relentless, as the arrows fell.

His thoughts turned, unbidden, to Elvira, his lady wife, her eyes brimming with grief as he had parted from her and their babe, Bohemond II, a child of mere moons when he set forth. The ache of that farewell cut deep—a father's love, a father's dread that he might never see his heir bear the name of Taranto with honor. War demanded its due. He knew it. He had known it when he pledged his sword to this cause. Savagery. Horror. He had witnessed it—villages sacked on their march through Anatolia, a woman and her child cast into flames by his own knights, her screams swallowed by the night. A pang of sorrow had struck him then, a fleeting doubt that clawed at his resolve. He buried it. They were infidels, foes of Christ, their doom just—or so he avowed. Yet the words rang hollow, for Bohemond knew the truth of his crusade: it was as much a quest for glory as for God, a chance to carve a kingdom, to outshine his father's deeds. Ambition—a fire that burned as fiercely as faith.

Another hail of arrows smote the shield-wall. Jarring. Fierce. The cries of his men—sharp, raw—as darts found their marks. Blood sprayed across his helm, a knight of Apulia fell, an arrow deep in his skull, body striking the earth with a dull thud. Bohemond and another closed the gap, shields locked, a bulwark 'gainst the storm. Behind, a mother's anguished plea for her wailing babe pierced the tumult. Clawing. Heart-wrenching. Bohemond steeled himself, mind bent on survival. Reinforcements were nigh—Raymond of Toulouse, his host, marching from the south. Yet Bohemond's trust in Raymond was scant. Old. Frail. The Count of Toulouse's zeal outstripped his vigor, and the Franks looked to Bohemond, not Raymond, to lead them to victory. The sun rose higher, its heat a scourge, but Bohemond would not let weariness show. He was their prince. Their warlord. He would not break—though the weight of his ambition, the blood it had cost, pressed heavy, a yoke he could not shed.

A sound. Faint. Swelling. Horns! The thunder of hooves! Bohemond's spirit surged, a fire kindled anew. "Stand firm!" he bellowed, voice rough, alive. "They come! Stand firm!" His men rallied, hearts lifted by hope. Bohemond gripped his blade, ready. The Seljuk arrows still fell, unyielding, but deliverance was at hand. Frankish cavalry burst forth, crashing into the Turkic ranks with mighty force, banners a blaze of color 'gainst the dust. Bohemond rose, shield aloft, blood aflame. A chance. A light in the darkness. "Deus vult!" he cried, voice soaring o'er the fray. "God wills it!" He charged, sword flashing in the sunlight, a warrior of the cross, driven by faith—and the unyielding ambition that had brought him to this blood-soaked field.

Kilij Arslan

The sun blazed fierce o'er the plains of Dorylaeum, a wrathful judge, its heat a scourge to all who stood beneath its unyielding gaze. Kilij Arslan, Sultan of the Seljuks of Rum, wiped sweat from his brow, his eyes—dark as the midnight steppe, keen as a falcon's—fixed upon the Frankish camp below. His brown steed, a noble beast of the Anatolian plains, stirred beneath him, restless, as if it sensed its master's disquiet. Arslan watched his bowmen loose another flight, shafts rising like a flock of deadly birds, their arc a grim omen 'gainst the sky, a harbinger of death for the invaders below.

These Franks, these crusaders, had come to his lands as a plague, their iron-shod hooves trampling the fields of Rum, their crosses a banner of conquest, dripping with the blood of his kin. They spake of a holy war, claiming the lands of Islam as their birthright, but Arslan saw their true visage—brigands, reavers, their piety a mask for greed. He had heard of their deeds: villages burned, children slain, mosques defiled by profane hands. His lip curled in scorn. The Franks sought not salvation, but dominion, their hunger for land a ravenous beast, insatiable as the desert sands that bordered his realm.

Arslan had been but a youth, scarce eighteen summers, when he took his father's throne—a realm fractured by the wars of old, conflicts with the Fatimids, the Byzantines, rival emirs of the East. The land of Rum was a tapestry of scars, its people weary of bloodshed, their eyes turned to him for hope. He was not his sire, a man broken by compromise, yielding to the Greeks at every turn. Young. Bold. Arslan had sworn to shield his folk from this tide of zealots, to forge a legacy that would endure, a name to echo through the ages. He had fought the Greeks at Nicaea, outwitting their emperor, Alexios Komnenos, though the city fell—a bitter loss. Now he faced these Franks, their numbers vast, their resolve unyielding, but

Arslan knew the ways of war, the swiftness of the steppe, the cunning of the desert. He would not yield his father's lands.

"Another flight, my lord?" Qutbuddin, his grizzled captain, rode nigh, voice sharp, eyes alight with the promise of battle.

"Aye," Arslan answered, tone steady as Konya's stone. "But venture not into open fray. Weary them. Let their strength bleed slow, as the desert wears the rock."

Qutbuddin paused, visage troubled, lines etched deep by years of war. "Strike now, and we might break them swiftly. A triumph to honor the Prophet, peace be upon him."

"And lose half our host for haste?" Arslan countered, gaze sharp as a scimitar's edge. "Nay, Qutbuddin. We hold the vantage—wield it with wisdom, not recklessness. The Franks are many, their hearts divided. Test their mettle. Break their spirit."

The captain bowed, though doubt lingered in his eyes, and rode to the bowmen, commands echoing o'er the din. Another storm of arrows took flight, a shadow o'er the field, falling with deadly precision. Arslan watched, the distant cries of the Franks hardening his heart. No delight in this slaughter. None. He was no butcher. Yet it was needful. These men had brought ruin—villages burned, innocents slain, holy places profaned. A blasphemy unanswerable. But a shadow crept into his soul—not of victory, but of cost. The Prophet, peace be upon him, spoke of mercy even in war, of life's sanctity. Did Allah will this carnage? Or had Arslan, in his zeal to defend his realm, strayed from the path? A question that lingered, heavy as the dust that choked the air.

The Franks had been caught unawares, their march halted by his sudden strike. Arslan had known of their coming since Nicaea fell—a loss that stung his pride, though he had withdrawn to fight another day. The Franks thought to divide their forces, to sweep through his lands ere he could muster his host, but Arslan had foreseen their plan, drawing on the wisdom of his ancestors, the swiftness of Seljuk horsemen. At Dorylaeum, the terrain favored his archers, pinning the Franks 'gainst the hills. A hunter's satisfaction, for the prey was cornered. Yet doubt gnawed—war, a fire consuming all, friend and foe alike, its flames indifferent to righteousness.

Qutbuddin returned, face set, voice low. "They weaken, my lord. Yet more Franks come—aid from the south." Arslan's jaw tightened. Mind racing. He had hoped to break them ere they could regroup, to spare his people further strife. But the Franks were stubborn, their allies likely led by a seasoned lord—Raymond of Toulouse, perhaps, or the Norman Tancred, Bohemond's kinsman. A harder fight loomed, a test of his resolve as much as theirs.

"Press them still," Arslan declared, voice firm as bedrock. "Harass them. Sap their spirit. We end this on our terms." Qutbuddin saluted, rode off. Arslan's thoughts whirled—stratagems, misgivings. Victory was near, a hunter's sense, but joyless. Hollow. War—a dance of death, a cycle sparing none, leaving only sorrow in its wake. He gazed upon the Franks, shields raised, visages pale, banners tattered. Foes.

Yes. But men—sons, fathers, bound by frail hopes as his own warriors. Both fought for faith, for home. What did it avail? Land? Might? Honor? Shadows, slipping through the grasp. Arslan wondered if his ambition—to hold Rum, to forge a legacy—had blinded him to the shared humanity beneath the clash. The Franks believed their God willed this war, as Arslan believed Allah guided his hand. Yet in the blood-soaked earth, the cries of the dying, he saw no divine will—only man's folly, pride a fire consuming all.

The sun dipped low, shadows stretching o'er the bloodied earth. Weariness settled upon Arslan, heavier than bone-ache. Fought for an age—Greeks, emirs, now Franks. Triumph near, but dust-tasting. "Let this be the end," he murmured to the wind, a vain hope. More battles. More wars. The world's cruel way, ever-turning, a cycle unbroken since the ancients. Horns! The earth trembled—Frankish horsemen, banners a blaze 'gainst the dust. Arslan's host stood firm, bows singing a deadly song. Armies clashed, steel ringing, a cacophony shaking the heavens. Arslan spurred his steed, joining the fray with a shout, scimitar flashing in the fading light. Skill. Precision. Yet the weight pressed—doubt, sorrow, lives lost to strife.

In the heat, foes blurred into marks, faces fading. But Arslan saw them—fear, whispered pleas to a far-off god, humanity laid bare in death. He fought on, driven by duty, teachings of youth, but doubt grew, a shadow unlifted. Righteousness? Honor? Or pride, a folly staining the earth with blood? The battle stretched into night, neither side yielding, a testament to stubborn faith, ambition. At last, the Franks broke, ranks crumbling, retreat a desperate flight. The field—strewn with fallen, Seljuk, Frank—the earth dark, air heavy with death's stench. Arslan stood at the edge, scimitar heavy, breath ragged, armor stained. Prevailed. No victory. Hollow. Grief—for the world, a place bound by hatred, endless strife.

He turned east, dawn's first light breaking, a pale promise unfulfilled. Sorrow gripped him, mourning not just the dead, but shared humanity lost in this clash of creeds. "Is this our lot?" he whispered, words lost, a plea to Allah, to the world, to the ghosts. "Slayers of men, driven by pride, faith, blind to mercy we profess?" The truth—a bitter draught, no solace. War, a cruel dance, claiming all, and mankind could not break free. Arslan mounted his steed, turning from carnage, questions heavy, a burden as great as the crown he bore. Fought for folk, faith, land, driven by a young man's ambition. Gained? Naught. Naught but blood, a legacy of sorrow.

PRISONER OF WAR

Section I: The Stille of Captivity

Snow fell soft and relentless from a firmament grey as forge-iron, cloaking the drear expanse of Stalag Luft III, a German prison camp nestled deep 'mongst the pine-shadowed wilds of Silesia. Here, in the frozen heart of the Reich, winter's bite was a merciless foe, its chill slicing through the threadbare garb of the captives like a dirk through parchment. The guards, perched in their turrets, rifles slung 'cross their breasts, gazed down with eyes shadowed 'neath steel helms—cold, unyielding, as if mercy had ne'er trod these lands. 'Twas December of the year 1944, and the world beyond these confines yet burned with the fires of war.

Arthur, an Allied airman, stood amidst the yard, shifting betwixt frost-numbed feet, his breath a fleeting wisp in the frigid air. About him gathered a motley host—Britons, Yankees, Canadians, with a scattering of Poles and Frenchmen, their loyalties unbowed though their wings were clipped. Shot down o'er France in 1942, Arthur had been snared by the foe, shuffled from camp to camp, each more desolate than the last, 'til he came to this icy purgatory. The men 'round him were but wraiths, their visages gaunt, eyes sunken as if the war had leached the very marrow from their bones, their uniforms tattered relics scarce fit to defy the winter's wrath.

The ground beneath was iron-hard, gripped by weeks of bitter frost, whilst snow clung to the barbed wire, shrouding the camp in a false serenity. Beyond these cruel bounds, the world blazed with strife—battlefields strewn 'cross Europa and the far Pacific, where men clashed and perished in droves. Yet here, all was muted, swallowed by the snow, as if even war's clamor could not pierce this forsaken stillness. A prison for soldiery alone, Stalag Luft III held no civilians, no Jews, no dissenters—only warriors, flyboys and footmen, officers and grunts, once soaring o'er enemy lines or charging into the fray, now reduced to mere ciphers, biding their days in silence.

Arthur's thoughts strayed, unbidden, to whispers of other camps—dark rumors of places where mercy was a myth, where suffering made even this frozen hell seem a boon. He shook his head, banishing such specters, striving to tether his mind to the present, to the yard where his fellow captives drifted like shades, heads bowed 'gainst the wind. Yet the thoughts lingered, haunting the long, quiet hours when darkness fell, a reminder of the fragility of their lot.

Three winters past had he last beheld her—Margaret, his heart's anchor. Three winters since he'd clasped her hand, heard her laughter, felt the warmth of her gaze. He let his eyes sweep the barren yard, as if her form might rise from the shadows, as if her memory alone could kindle a flame in this place where warmth was but a dream. Margaret. Her name, a talisman, summoned visions of a life unmarred by war—a life of gentle dawns, her hair a cascade of chestnut, her smile a beacon. Three winters since he'd left her at their threshold, her eyes glistening with unshed tears, a brave smile upon her lips as he marched to war, vowing to return 'ere the year's end.

Yet years had unfurled, an endless skein of days bleeding into nights, seasons shifting 'midst the camp's unchanging bleakness, 'til time itself seemed a phantom. Each morn mirrored the last—chill, still, void. Margaret's memory was his sole tether, a reminder that he was yet a man, not merely another hollow gaze lost to the frost. Her words, oft repeated in their sunlit days, echoed now in his mind: "Strength and patience, Arthur. Those twain shall bear thee through all trials." A mantra, a lodestone, grounding him 'midst the desolation.

He drew his hands deeper into his sleeves, fingers stiff, knuckles raw and fissured from the frost's cruel embrace. Numbness had crept into his very bones, a creeping malaise he scarce noted now. The men 'round him moved as specters, breath rising in fleeting clouds, dissipating into the icy air—a silent testament to their endurance, their refusal to yield. Arthur closed his eyes, summoning her visage, her laughter a melody that once filled their humble abode, a warmth to defy the chill that sought to claim him.

Section II: Life Before War

The barracks loomed, a warren of souls pressed shoulder to shoulder on narrow wooden bunks, the air thick with the reek of damp wool, unwashed flesh, and the faint tang of sickness. Thin boards, their grain warped by frost, offered scant shield 'gainst the winter's bite, the wind's howl a mournful dirge that rattled the timbers. Arthur curled upon his bunk, knees to chest, arms clasped tight, seeking warmth in his own frame. Without, the gale raged, a banshee's wail that sent shivers through the huddled men, a reminder of their frailty.

A lone bulb, its light wan and flickering, hung from the ceiling, casting ghostly shadows upon the faces of his fellows—each man a study in privation, lost in his own torment, scarce speaking, seeking a corner of the mind untainted by hardship. Arthur felt his spirit wane, dragged low by hunger's gnaw, the frost's embrace, the silence that pressed like a stone. Eyes closed, he fled to memory, to a time when warmth was no myth, when Margaret's presence was a balm 'gainst the world's storms.

In his mind's eye, he stood anew in their modest dwelling, a haven of sunlight where they'd woven the tapestry of their early wedded days. There she was, vivid as a summer's morn, stirring a pot on the stove, her dark tresses curling 'round her face, laughter spilling forth like a brook's song. A summer's day, light streaming through the casement, curtains dancing in the breeze. She glanced o'er her shoulder, a teasing smile upon her lips, catching him in his gaze—a moment of joy, unmarred by the specter of war.

They'd wed young, scarce more than bairns in a world vast and daunting, yet fear had not touched them. Each day a gift, filled with simple delights—a picnic by the river's edge, Margaret spreading a blanket, her hands deft as she carved the bread, their laughter mingling with the sun's descent. Hours spent in idle talk, dreams spilling forth like wine, the world a canvas of possibility. Her hand in his, soft, sure—a tether he'd ne'er thought to lose. Here, in this frozen void, that touch was a lifeline, a memory he clutched with a ferocity born of desperation.

A breath, shaky, as he whispered her name—Margaret—soft as a prayer, lest the others hear. Her scent, lavender and sunlight, lingered in his mind, a ghost of days when she moved through their home, humming a tune that wrapped 'round him, a melody of peace. Nights in their parlor, furniture pushed aside, dancing with clumsy grace—her laughter as they spun, dizzy, her head on his shoulder, breath warm 'gainst his neck. No skill had he, yet with her, it mattered not. They swayed, heartbeats in rhythm, a sanctuary 'midst a world soon to shatter.

Yet memory was a double-edged blade, its warmth a solace, its edge a torment. How true were these visions? Did he gild the past, smoothing its rough edges 'til only golden light remained? Perchance. Yet what else had he to cling to, to keep from sinking into the hollow-eyed despair that claimed so many 'round him? Doubt crept in, a shadow o'er his heart—did Margaret yet recall him, after three winters' silence? Had she forsaken their vow, made on the morn of his departure? He'd vanished 'cross the sea, leaving her to wait, to wonder, with naught but silence to answer her fears.

Section III: The Reaper's Chill

Winter was a living fiend in Stalag Luft III, slithering through every chink and crevice, a relentless foe that gnawed at flesh and bone, a second skin none could shed. E'en within the barracks, the thin walls offered scant reprieve, the stoves—when lit—casting a feeble glow that warmed only those nearest, leaving the far bunks to shiver. Men huddled 'neath blankets, threadbare and coarse, bodies pressed close for what meager heat they might share. Futile. The chill found them all, unyielding as the Reich's iron grip.

Days bled into one another, a dreary litany. Dawn brought the same cruel rite: roll call. Guards burst in, barking in guttural German, voices sharp as the frost, rousing the men from fitful slumber. Groggy, trembling, they stumbled without, forming ragged lines, breaths misting in the icy air as they stood, silent, still, to be tallied. The guards paced, eyes narrowed, rifles poised. A twitch, a misstep—swift rebuke, or worse. So they stood, thin frames rigid, toes and fingers numbing, as the count dragged on, oft for naught but cruelty's sake, 'til the cold seeped into their very souls.

After, they were herded back, awaiting rations—a crust of stale bread, a broth thin as gruel, tasteless as ash. Arthur's mind drifted to Margaret's table—stews rich with warmth, bread fresh from the oven, her soft hum as she served. Now, hunger was a constant specter, a gnawing void that sapped their strength. Men withered, frames gaunt, cheeks sunken, eyes dimming. E'en simple tasks left them breathless, and the sick—those who fell—rarely rose again.

Arthur strove to keep his wits, to move, to endure, but the frost made all a torment—joints aching, muscles leaden, as if his body forgot its purpose. He saw it in the others: the shuffle of their steps, shoulders bowed, gazes vacant—soldiers once proud, now shades, half-buried in despair. Some ceased to speak, their voices as lost as their hope. A quiet surrender, a creeping doom that chilled Arthur more than the frost. He fought it, clinging to Margaret's memory, her words a shield: *Strength and patience.*

One eve, as he gnawed a crust, a wet, racking cough shattered the stillness. Across the barracks, Davis—a Yankee flyer, steadfast 'til now—huddled on his bunk, visage flushed, sweat beading despite the chill. Arthur had known him but a few moons, yet Davis's quiet fortitude had been a bulwark 'gainst the camp's despair. Now, he seemed a frail wight, shivering 'neath his blanket, each cough a dagger to the silence.

The men nigh him shifted, drawing back, eyes flickering with dread and pity. Sickness was a plague here, swift to spread, deadly in its grip. The guards cared not—medics were scarce, supplies a jest: a handful of aspirin, a scrap of gauze. No miracles dwelt in this forsaken place. Over days, Arthur watched Davis fade, his cough a death knell, his frame curling inward, skin pale, damp with fever. Arthur offered what he could—water, a crust when the guards' eyes were elsewhere—but it availed little. Davis's gaze held resignation, a slow yielding to the reaper's call.

The guards, as ever, were indifferent, their glances cold as the frost that rimed the walls. Another sick man—a burden eased, a mouth less to feed. Arthur's fists clenched, rage a bitter fire 'gainst his helplessness. He could not save Davis, could not ease the anguish in his friend's eyes. So he watched, each cough a shared wound, fear sinking deep—a harbinger of his own fragility.

Davis slipped away on a morn of bitter frost, breaths shallow, then still, eyes fixed on a realm beyond. The guards came, lifting him as if he were naught, hauling him forth with a carelessness that seared Arthur's heart. The men watched, mute, gazes downcast. No words. No name spoken. Easier to let him fade, a shadow lost to memory. Yet Arthur felt the void, a wound that gnawed in the quiet hours, a dread that he, too, might vanish thus, a name on a list, a shade in the frost.

He resolved then to defy the reaper's chill. He could not save Davis, but he could fight for the living. The barracks—riven with gaps, the wind's cruel ingress—needed mending. After roll call, he scavenged: scraps of paper, tatters of cloth, straw gleaned from the yard when the guards' eyes strayed. He stuffed the chinks, each scrap a bulwark 'gainst the frost, a small defiance. At first, the others watched, bemused, but soon some joined, offering bits of rag, a shared labor 'gainst the cold. A frail hope, yet it kindled a fire within them—a purpose, a stand 'gainst despair.

Section IV: The Letter Exchange

Rumors flitted through the camp, a quiet hum, electric, passing bunk to bunk in hushed murmurs, wary glances. A guard's careless word, a prisoner's ear bent nigh the wire—an exchange of missives, perchance, brokered by the Red Cross. Some scoffed, naming it a fool's dream, a mirage born of longing. Yet for the first time in moons, there was talk—hope, fragile as a sparrow's wing, stirring the men from their stupor.

Arthur heard the whispers, sitting upright, a flicker of warmth blooming within, unlinked to the scraps he'd stuffed 'gainst the frost. A letter exchange. He mouthed the words, tasting their weight, as if utterance might summon their truth. Could Margaret have penned a note, her script a lifeline 'cross the void? Or news of the Allies' advance, liberation nigh? Hope, a dangerous flame, flared bright, unquenchable.

Days stretched, taut with anticipation, unease. Men spake in low tones, wary of the guards' ears, each caught 'twixt hope and dread, a mirror to Arthur's own turmoil. Peril lay in hoping overmuch, yet he could not stem the tide—visions of her words, a scrap of her to hold, or tidings of freedom. The barracks buzzed, men's eyes alight, some daring to speak of home, of kin, of dreams beyond the wire—a spark to defy the chill, if but for a moment.

Arthur felt a fool, clinging to such a wisp. No word had come since his capture, though Red Cross parcels oft bore letters for others—precious scraps, lines from a wife, a child, a dam. Some brought joy, softening a man's visage, kindling light in his eyes. Others bore sorrow, lines deepening, gazes fixed on words unseen. A letter could heal—or wound deeper than steel. Yet Arthur yearned to be among them, to hold news of Margaret, e'en if it bore pain.

Waiting became a torment, seeping into his thoughts, filling the void. Footsteps without, a guard's passing, a distant shout—each quickened his pulse, eyes darting, hope rising, falling. He was not alone. The men shared his restlessness, their stoic masks cracking, voices rising in tentative dreams. But each day sans word brought fear—what if naught came? What if Margaret had not written, or could not? The thought twisted, a blade sharper than frost, a darkness he durst not face.

A few letters trickled in, each a pang to Arthur's heart, hopes soaring, crashing. Some men read with quiet joy, eyes alight with home's memory. Others folded their missives, faces blank, retreating to shadowed corners, bearing silent wounds. Letters—rare relics, shared 'mongst the men, a reminder of the world beyond. Yet for each who received, many waited in vain, visages tightening, eyes dimming, hope fading with the frost.

Weeks passed, the rumor fading, replaced by whispers of battles—victories, losses, lands freed or held. The letters ne'er came, a promise turned to smoke, a cruel jest. Arthur felt the sting, a raw ache hollowing him, the hope he'd nurtured now a bitter jest. Yet in that void, a clarity bloomed—he needed not a letter to hold Margaret near. Her memory, her words, were etched within, a fire no frost could quench. He resolved to endure, to fight, to live—not for a missive, but for the chance to return to her, to prove her faith not in vain.

Section V: Strength and Patience

Arthur sat solitary in the barracks' dim gloaming, back pressed 'gainst the rough-hewn wall, knees hugged tight to his chest, the frost slithering through every chink like a thief in the night. Yet tonight, the chill was the least of his foes. Margaret's words, his beacon in the blackest hours, echoed soft and faint in his mind: *Strength and patience, Arthur. Those two things will carry you through anything.* Her voice, steady as a hearth's glow, had calmed him in their sunlit days back home—a charm against the world's storms. Here, 'midst the camp's shadows, they were his shield 'gainst despair. But tonight, they slipped, a melody half-forgotten, a lifeline fraying in his grasp.

A low, guttural sound—a groan, raw and heavy— pierced his reverie. Across the bunk, Carter, a Brit pilot who'd always kept to himself, slumped with his head bowed, hands clenched so tight his knuckles gleamed white in the faint light. Quiet, sure, but tonight his silence carried a weight that seemed to crush him. Arthur shifted, leaning forward, his voice soft, cautious. "Carter. You holding up, mate?"

No answer at first, Carter's shoulders rigid, hands locked in a vise. Then, slowly, he lifted his head, eyes hollow, red-rimmed, the kind of hollow that spoke of nights without sleep, days without hope. "Holding up?" he muttered, voice thick, bitter as the camp's watery soup. "What's that even mean anymore? We're here, freezing our bones, eating slop, waiting for a day that might never come."

Arthur nodded, the weight of Carter's words hitting like a punch, a mirror to his own dark thoughts. "I get it," he said quietly, voice low but steady. "I've had those days myself—days where it feels like the walls are closing in. But we're still here, Carter. We've made it this far. That's something."

Carter shook his head, a laugh escaping him—sharp, jagged, like glass breaking. "Made it?" His voice cracked, and he looked away, staring at some unseen point in the shadows. "This isn't making it, Arthur. This is… nothing. My wife—she's probably moved on by now. Can't say I blame her. What am I to her anymore? A ghost?"

Arthur felt a pang, sharp and cold, the echo of his own fears—did Margaret still wait, still hold him in her heart after three long winters? He pushed the thought down, focusing on Carter, on the man crumbling before him. "Listen to me," he said, voice firm now, cutting through the gloom. "You don't know that for sure. You don't know what's happening out there, beyond the wire."

Carter's gaze snapped back, bleak as the Silesian frost. "Maybe not," he said, voice dropping to a murmur, raw with pain. "But I can feel myself slipping away, Arthur. Every day, there's less of me. What's the point of holding on when there's nothing left to hold onto?"

Arthur leaned closer, eyes steady, unyielding, his voice a quiet anchor in the dark. "The point is to keep going, Carter. To get through each day, one at a time. To hold on because it's all we've got—it's all we can control." He paused, Margaret's words rising within him, a steady flame against the chill. "When I get those days—when it feels like too much—I think of something my wife used to say. She'd tell me, 'Strength and patience. Those two things will carry you through anything.'"

Carter's brow furrowed, his voice bitter, almost mocking. "Strength and patience?" he echoed, the words heavy with doubt. "And what good has that done you here, in this frozen hell?"

Arthur held his gaze, unflinching, his voice low but sure, a quiet conviction born of survival. "It's kept me alive, hasn't it?" he said simply. "It's kept me holding on, day after day. That's something, Carter. That's everything." He softened, his tone gentling, reaching out across the shadowed space between them. "You hold on to what you've got—to the people you love, even if they feel like a memory. Even if the world tries to tell you they're gone."

Carter's eyes flickered, a faint glimmer of light breaking through the despair, a sign he was listening, taking it in. "And what if she has moved on?" he asked, voice breaking, the question a wound laid bare. "What if I'm just holding onto something that's already gone?"

Arthur took a slow breath, Margaret's face steadying him—her smile, her warmth, her laughter—a vision that had carried him through the darkest nights. "Then we keep holding on anyway," he said softly, each word measured, heavy with truth. "Because those memories, those feelings—they're part of us. They've shaped who we are, made us who we are. We carry them with us, no matter where we end up. And if we make it out of here—if we get to see them again—that's a gift worth fighting for. But even if we don't, we carry them forward, keep them alive in us."

Carter fell silent, his expression unreadable at first, but there was a softening in his gaze, a hint that Arthur's words had taken root. "You make it sound simple," he murmured after a long pause, his voice quieter now, less bitter, though still heavy with the weight of their reality. "But it's not, is it?"

"No," Arthur admitted, his voice gentle, honest. "It's not. There are days when it feels impossible—days when I don't even know if I believe it myself. But it's all we've got, Carter. Strength and patience. One step, one day at a time."

A stillness settled between them, warm despite the frost, each man retreating into his own thoughts, his own memories. Arthur felt a calm wash over him, a peace he hadn't known in months—he realized then that Margaret's love, even across the endless miles, had sustained him. Strength and patience. They had carried him this far, through the cold, the hunger, the despair, and they would carry him further still, until he could hold her again.

Arthur leaned back against the wall, letting that thought settle deep, a quiet fire to warm him through the night. Strength and patience, he repeated to himself, the words solid, real, an anchor in the storm. They had been enough to see him through, and they would be enough to carry him home—one day at a time.

THE TAMING OF THE BARD

I stood upon the theatre's weathered stage, the late afternoon sun pouring through the open roof, roasting me in my woollen doublet as though I were a goose trussed for a feast. Sweat trickled down my neck, the coarse fabric scratching like a thousand nettles, but I durst not stir—not with Master William Shakespeare perched upon a stool five paces hence, his quill dripping ink upon the boards, his gaze sharp enough to flay a man's soul. 'Twas the year of our Lord 1594, and I, Thomas Harker, a lad of nineteen summers and greener than a May sapling, had somehow found myself amidst the Chamberlain's Men, the finest company of players in all of London.

We'd been at it since the noon bell, the company weary from a morning of *Richard III*, and now we were deep in rehearsal for *The Taming of the Shrew*, set to open on the morrow. I bore the weighty role of Petruchio—my first true part, my one chance to prove I belonged amongst these giants. A painted cloth of Padua hung crookedly above, a boy sweeping straw from the boards, and the empty benches stared down, a silent jury awaiting my verdict. Yet standing there, I felt more a fool in a pillory than a leading man.

"Again, Thomas!" Master Shakespeare bellowed, his voice a mingle of honeyed charm and stinging nettles, the sort that could woo a lady or whip a knave. His auburn beard quivered, his doublet a fine green that made my patched hose seem the garb of a beggar. "And this time, give me fire, not dung! 'I'll curb her mad and headstrong humour'—thou'rt wooing a shrew, not a milkmaid in a meadow!"

He was not merely the playmaker; he was the master of this wooden O, a guiding hand who had penned *Shrew* to outshine the Admiral's Men, our rivals at the Rose, and he would suffer no imperfection—even if it meant breaking me like a colt to the bridle. "I'd see if this lad hath fire to match Petruchio's!" he muttered, his eyes glinting with mischief, and I felt my innards twist—*I'd dreamt of this stage's life, not it's scythe.*

I cleared my throat, the line lodged in my gullet like a fishbone. "I'll curb her mad and headstrong humour," I ventured, striving to growl as Petruchio ought, but my voice broke upon "humour," turning it to a squeak more befitting a mouse than a man.

Richard Burbage, the company's brightest star, playing Katherina, adjusted his corset with a grimace, his wig making him more vulture than lady, and smirked from the wings. "Fresh meat for the Bard's quern," he muttered, loud enough for mine ears to catch, his desire for the stage's light dimmed by my blundering. The company—ten men strewn about the stage, mending props or murmuring lines—burst into guffaws.

"Zounds, boy!" Shakespeare leapt from his stool, ink splattering like a soldier's blood upon the boards. "Thou soundest as a plowman cooing to a cow! More fire, less filth!" He strode toward me, his boots thumping the stage, and thrust a rolled manuscript under my nose, the parchment reeking of fresh ink and wax. "Petruchio is a lion, Thomas, not a mewling kitten. Give me a roar that shakes these timbers!"

I nodded, my cheeks aflame beneath the doublet's torment, and tried once more. "I'll curb her mad and headstrong humour!" I cried, but my arms hung stiff, and my tone sounded more a tavern braggart than a fiery suitor.

Shakespeare flung up his hands, his quill sailing across the stage to land in a heap of straw. "Nay, nay, nay! Where's the passion? Where's the swagger? Petruchio must rule the stage, not totter like a tosspot!" He seized my shoulders, his grip as iron, and spun me to face the empty benches. "Behold them, Thomas—the groundlings, the lords, even Hunsdon himself, our noble patron, awaiting to see if we be worth his gold. Thou'lt not make me the jest of Shoreditch!"

His voice dropped, a glint in his eye that bespoke mischief. "Now, try again—and this time, flourish thy cape as a Spanish matador, laugh as a corsair who hath plundered a galleon, and sneer as a knave who hath filched a rival's purse."

I blinked, my wits a muddle. Flourish my cape? Laugh like a corsair? Sneer? I scarce knew the lines, let alone how to juggle such feats. But I could not gainsay him—not Master Shakespeare, not with the company's eyes upon me, not with my first role hanging by a thread. I adjusted my cape, a moth-eaten rag the wardrobe lad had unearthed from a musty trunk, and gave it a swing. The fabric caught on my belt, yanking me sideways, and I stumbled into a prop table. A wooden cup, a tin plate, and a false apple clattered to the stage, rolling into the yard where a stagehand, a gangly boy named Ned, scrambled to catch them.

The company roared with mirth, Burbage loudest, his wig slipping as he clutched his sides.

I felt my innards twist, the jest stinging worse than the doublet's itch, and I longed to prove myself, to earn their good opinion, to show I belonged amidst these legends. I righted myself, brushing straw from my hose, and ad-libbed, "My Petruchio courts with fire, not kisses!" hoping to win a smile, but Shakespeare's eyes narrowed. "Fire, sayest thou? Thou'rt more smoke than flame!" he retorted, his voice a whip, and the company sniggered anew.

"Enough!" Shakespeare cried, his face redder than a Southwark bawd's cheeks. "This rabble will undo my genius! Thomas, thou'rt a calamity in boots!"

He paced, stroking his beard, then snapped his fingers with a grin that made my stomach sink. "When thou speakest 'headstrong humour,' I would have thee leap upon yon barrel"—he pointed to a prop in the corner, a stout cask meant to stand for Petruchio's table—"and crow as a rooster who hath just claimed the henhouse. That shall show Petruchio's spirit!"

Will Kempe, the company's jester, piped up, mimicking a rooster's crow with a flapping of his arms. "Cock-a-doodle-doo! Let the lad crow, Will!" he cried, his grin wide, and the company laughed, Kempe's jest stoking their mirth.

I trudged to the barrel, my doublet itching worse with every step, and climbed up, my boots slipping on the wood. I opened my mouth to crow, but my foot caught the edge, and I toppled backward, landing flat on my back with a thud that echoed through the Theatre.

The company howled, Kempe doubling over, and Ned dropped a plank in his laughter. Shakespeare sighed, pinching the bridge of his nose, but a chuckle escaped him. "Perchance there's mettle in this mud," he muttered, stepping over to offer a hand, his grin returning. "Better, lad, but not yet a jewel. Let us try once more."

I took his hand, hauling myself up, my back throbbing, my pride bruised worse than my bones. But that grin—rare as a fair day in London—kindled a fire in me. I'd show him I belonged, even if it meant crowing like a rooster or sneering like a cutpurse.

Shakespeare turned to the company, his voice booming. "A duel of wits, then! Thomas, when thou speakest 'I'll curb her,' thou shalt challenge Burbage as though he were a rival suitor, and let thy words be thy lance!" He tossed me a prop sword, its wooden blade chipped, and I caught it, my hands trembling. A duel? I'd scarce held a blade, but I nodded, determined to please him.

I strode toward Burbage, who adjusted his wig with a sneer, and shouted, "I'll curb her mad and headstrong humour, thou vulture in a petticoat!"

The company gasped, then laughed, Burbage's face reddening beneath his rouge. "Vulture, sayest thou?" he retorted, drawing his own prop sword. "I'll tame thee first, thou crowing coxcomb!"

We sparred with words, not blades, my line—"My Kate shall bend, or I'll break her!"—met by his—"I'll break thee first, thou prancing fool!" The company cheered, Kempe shouting, "A battle of wits, and both unarmed!" I felt a spark— I'd turned their laughter to my side, if only for a moment. *I'd not be written off—not by the Bard himself,* I thought, my heart swelling. Tomorrow was the debut, and I'd make Petruchio roar, Master Shakespeare's whims be damned.

The Theatre thrummed with life on opening night, the yard a sea of groundlings—fishwives, apprentices, and rogues in tattered cloaks—pressed shoulder-to-shoulder, while the galleries above held nobles in velvet doublets, their eyes keen with expectation. A lute player struck a jaunty tune from the shadows, and a boy lit torches to cast a golden glow as the night deepened, a painted cloth of Padua shifting to reveal the scene.

I stepped onto the stage, my boots creaking on the weathered boards, my woollen doublet still chafing from yesterday's ordeal. The air buzzed with shouts, the scent of ale and unwashed bodies rising from the crowd, and I felt the promise of this night—a chance to prove I belonged, to turn the lessons of Master Shakespeare's chaotic rehearsal into triumph.

He watched from the wings, his quill tucked behind his ear, his green doublet catching the torchlight, his gaze a storm I now met with a nod. I opened with Petruchio's first speech—"Verona, for a while I take my leave"—my voice steady, the words flowing as I'd practiced through the night.

When Petruchio's line came—"I'll curb her mad and headstrong humour"—I crowed as a rooster who hath claimed the henhouse, just as Master Shakespeare had demanded in rehearsal. My voice rang out, a hearty "Cock-a-doodle-doo!" that sent the groundlings into peals of laughter, a fishwife shouting, "Petruchio's a right fowl suitor!"

I bowed low, the cheers washing over me, a balm to yesterday's bruises, and I knew I'd turned Master Shakespeare's jibe to my gain. *I'd dreamt of crowing as a fool, but now I crow as a player,* I thought, my heart swelling with the crowd's mirth.

Burbage strode forth as Katherina, his wig a-tilt, adjusting his corset with a grimace, and cut in with a dramatic outburst—"I'll tame thee with my scorn, thou rooster!" The crowd gasped, then cheered, their eyes on him, and I saw his smirk, his desire to dim my light burning bright.

I'd not let him best me—not after yesterday's trials. "Good Kate, my scorn's sharper than thy tongue!" I ad-libbed, and the groundlings roared, a noble tossing a penny that glinted as it landed.

A pockmarked man with a tankard heckled, "Methinks Petruchio's more fool than suitor!" The crowd laughed, and I felt the sting, my doublet itching worse under their jeers.

Master Shakespeare's voice cut through, sharp as a blade. "Thomas, a duel of wits—now!" he cried from the wings, his arm waving as though directing a siege.

I seized a prop staff, my arm steadier than yesterday, and thrust it as though I were a knight at a tourney, bellowing, "I'll have no wife but one who bends!" The crowd cheered, and I saw Master Shakespeare pause, then laugh—a rare nod that lit a fire in me.

"Perchance this lad hath wit I scarce foresaw," he muttered, and strode onto the stage, his boots a thunderclap, striking a pose. "Fool, sayest thou? I'll play Hortensio—'I promised we would be contributors'—and steal thy shrew!"

The crowd gasped, then cheered, thinking 'twas part of the play, Hortensio giving Petruchio a lift to win the shrew, and I saw Burbage's glare, his spotlight stolen once more. Master Shakespeare turned to me, his eyes glinting with mischief. "Woo thy Kate, Petruchio—I'll bear thy charge of wooing, whatsoe'er!"

I bowed low, my mind a whirl, but the crowd's cheers spurred me on. "Fair Hortensio, my Kate tames all—even scribbling knaves!" I thrust the staff in a mock challenge, and Master Shakespeare danced aside, his laughter a melody.

"I'll wager my quill she'll choose a poet!" he countered, and the groundlings roared, a noble in the gallery shouting, "A purse for Hortensio—I'd see him win the shrew!"

The crowd cheered, thinking the noble meant Master Shakespeare, and he played along, bowing low. "My lord, I'll take thy purse—but Petruchio must yield!" he cried, prompting a fishwife to shout, "Nay, let the rooster fight!"

A groundling, thinking the noble's purse a real wager, tossed a cabbage at Master Shakespeare, shouting, "Win thy shrew, Hortensio!" Master Shakespeare dodged, but slipped on the cabbage, landing on his backside with a thud. The crowd howled, and I ad-libbed, "My Kate tames cabbages and poets alike!"

The groundlings cheered louder, a boy yelling, "Encore for the rooster!" Burbage, seeing the tide turn, flounced forth as Katherina. "I'll have neither of ye—I'll tame ye both!" he cried—his wig flying into the yard, caught by a fishwife who waved it like a banner.

Kempe leapt in, his jester's grin wide, dancing a jig around Burbage. "Methinks Katherina's a wilder shrew than e'er I dreamed!" he cried, and the crowd roared, their cheers a thunder.

The play stumbled to its end—"My hand is ready; may it do him ease!"—and the applause thundered, groundlings stomping, nobles clapping, Hunsdon's stern face breaking into a smile from the gallery, a noble shouting, "Encore for the Bard!" I took my bow, my hose still damp, my doublet a torment, but my chest alight with triumph. *I'd feared his quill would write me out, but now he writes me in,* I thought, the crowd's cheers a balm to my pride.

Master Shakespeare clapped me on the shoulder, his grin wide. "Thou'rt a player, Thomas—a fool, but a player true. We've made a triumph of this chaos." He saluted the crowd, a spark of his charm lighting the night, and I knew I'd earned my place—not through perfection, but through grit and a jest.

The Chamberlain's Men gathered in the tiring-house after, a painted cloth of Padua shifting behind us as a boy doused the torches. We passed a jug of ale, their toasts a balm to my pride.

Burbage raised his cup, his smirk softened to a nod. "To Petruchio, the Foolish Knight—thou'st a fire I'll not quench," he said, and the company laughed, their eyes holding a new respect.

Kempe slapped my back, his jester's grin wide. "Thou'rt one of us, lad—wet hose and all." I drank deep, the ale warm in my throat, and felt the Theatre's timbers hum around me. *I'd come to prove myself, and found a fellowship instead—* my first victory, won through chaos and a smile, on a stage that now called me its own.

A NEW LEGACY

A Neo Haven Short Story, 2095

The Council Hall loomed as a cold monolith, its steel walls polished to a quicksilver gleam, a testament to Neo Haven's technocratic gods—men and women who wielded data like blades, slicing the city's future into neat, obedient lines. Massive holo-displays pulsed along the chamber, streams of real-time metrics flickering—crime rates, resource quotas, dissent indices—each digit a shackle binding the city's pulse. The air buzzed with clipped voices, sharp and efficient, as Council members, corporate titans, and Upper City elites glided through the throng, their tailored suits and cybernetic implants glinting under the sterile light, every gesture weighted with the arrogance of those who believed they carried Neo Haven's fate alone.

Lukas Tellar lingered at the room's edge, a champagne flute clutched in his hand, the glass slick with condensation, its bubbles rising slow and indifferent to the storm roiling in his chest. He'd mastered these galas—smiles tight, nods precise, the dutiful son of Baron Tellar, Council luminary—but the act chafed raw tonight, an invisible chain cinching tighter with every forced nod. His father stood at the chamber's heart, a colossus in black, his voice booming smooth and commanding from the podium, extolling the city's latest triumph: a predictive surveillance algorithm, *All-Seeing Eye 2.0*, designed to tighten the Council's grip on Neo Haven's underbelly, rooting out dissent before it could spark. "Our brightest minds," Baron declared, his piercing gray eyes sweeping the crowd, landing heavy on Lukas, "have ensured our city's order. I salute my son, Lukas Tellar, whose tireless work has made this possible. He is—mark my words—the future of Neo Haven."

Polite applause rippled, hands clapping like synchronized drones, and Lukas forced a smile—lips thin, eyes dead—as the crowd turned to him, their gazes assessing, weighing, judging. Baron's praise was a noose, silk-smooth but strangling, each word knotting tighter around his neck. He nodded slight, the motion mechanical, the weight of expectation crashing down—a legacy he'd carried since he could walk, a path carved in steel he hadn't chosen. His father beamed, pride radiating like heat from a forge, reveling in this moment—the Tellar name a pillar of Neo Haven's might, Lukas its heir, bound to uphold it without question.

The applause faded, conversations resuming in efficient murmurs, and Lukas felt the familiar vise grip his chest, air thinning in his lungs. He wasn't new to this role—junior analyst, Council prodigy, heir apparent—but every glowing word from Baron's mouth buried him deeper, suffocating a self he barely knew. Excusing himself from a knot of corporate suits—*"Fine work, Tellar,"* one droned, cyber-eye whirring—he slipped toward the hall's rear, movements deliberate but swift, weaving through the crowd with practiced ease, though he felt their eyes—sharp, evaluative—tracking his retreat. The steel doors swung open, and he stepped into the night, rain pattering soft against the pavement, a cool balm on his skin that eased the pressure in his chest, if only a fraction.

Neo Haven's skyline glittered before him, a labyrinth of glass spires and neon veins, its Upper City towers piercing the clouds, their sleek lines a lie of beauty masking the machine beneath—cold, calculated, relentless in its hunger for control. The Old City sprawled below, a festering wound of rust and ash, its rad-zones glowing faint where the '52 meltdown had scarred the earth, its people scrabbling in the Council's shadow. Lukas stood still, letting the rain soak his shirt, the droplets weaving paths down his face. Baron's voice echoed—*"The future of this city"*—but it wasn't his future. He didn't want this cage, this machine that ground lives to dust under the guise of order. He craved something else—freedom, maybe, or truth— but its shape eluded him, a shadow flickering just out of reach.

Glancing back at the hall's doors, their steel gleam taunting, he saw the life waiting inside: more praise, more chains, more of Baron's vision swallowing him whole. With a breath sharp as a blade, Lukas turned and walked away, rain mixing with the city's hum, his steps carrying him deeper into the dark, away from his father's shadow, toward a path he couldn't yet see.

Lukas trudged through Neo Haven's underbelly, the Upper City's polished spires giving way to the Old City's crumbling sprawl, where streets sagged under the weight of decay, their asphalt pocked and split, choked with ash and twisted rebar. The air thickened here, heavy with ozone and sweat, the neon signs flickering weak—pink, green, their buzz a faint pulse against the drone of distant machinery. Laborers shuffled past, faces gaunt, cyber-limbs creaking under patched coats, their coughs hacking loud in the damp chill, while drones hummed overhead, their red lenses scanning, ever-watchful, the Council's eyes in the sky. Lukas pulled his collar tight, dodging a patrol drone's sweep, its beam slicing the alley's gloom, his heart ticking fast as he slipped into a narrower path, the walls closing in—graffiti-smeared, rust weeping down their seams like blood from old wounds.

He reached a tucked-away café, its sign half-dark, *"Neon Brew"* blinking faint in the haze, a sanctuary from the city's gaze. The door creaked as he pushed through, the scent of spiced coffee and worn leather flooding his senses, warm and grounding, a stark contrast to the Council Hall's sterile chill. Patrons dotted the room—shadowed figures hunched over mugs, their faces obscured in the neon's dim glow, low murmurs weaving through the air like static. Lukas spotted Juno at the back, her dark eyes catching his with a quiet intensity that pierced him, seeing through the mask he'd worn all night, peeling back the dutiful son to the raw, restless core beneath.

"Rough one?" she asked, voice soft but keen, sliding a steaming mug toward him as he sank into the chair across from her, the wood creaking under his weight.

He gripped the mug tight, its warmth seeping into his palms, but it couldn't touch the storm twisting inside—Baron's words, *"The future of this city"*, a chain he couldn't break. "Same old," he muttered, voice low and jagged, staring into the coffee's dark swirl. "Another gala, another speech—me as the Tellar heir, Neo Haven's next big hope, all laid out like it's written in stone."

Juno leaned back, arms folding across her chest, her leather jacket creaking faint, her gaze unreadable but piercing. "You don't sound sold," she said, a dry edge to her tone, her fingers tapping soft against her sleeve, a rhythm that matched the rain's patter outside.

"I'm not," Lukas admitted, the words spilling heavy, his voice cracking faint as he met her eyes, dark and steady, a mirror to his own doubt. "Never was, maybe. It's all planned— analyst, Council seat, Tellar legacy—like I'm just a cog slotted in, no say, no out. Every step I take, it's his path, not mine."

She tilted her head, a strand of black hair falling loose, her voice softening but firm. "You don't have to walk it, Lukas. You know that, don't you? You can break the damn mold— carve your own way, whatever it looks like."

He shook his head sharp, frustration gnawing deep, his knuckles whitening around the mug. "Not that easy," he said, voice tight and low, the words bitter as the coffee. "You don't get it—Baron's not just my father, he's the Council's fist. The Tellar name—it's everything I am, everything I've been shaped to be. If I turn my back, I'm not just leaving him—I'm torching who I am, what I've got left."

Juno's eyes flickered—empathy, frustration, something fiercer—and she leaned forward, her hand resting light on his, a warmth that jolted him, steady and real. "You're not torching yourself if you choose different," she said, voice fierce now, cutting through the café's hum. "You're finding who you are— outside his shadow, outside that machine. Staying loyal to a name that's choking you, that's the real betrayal—of you."

Her words hit like a shock, raw and true, and Lukas held her gaze, feeling the weight of her hand, the honesty in her stare, a shift stirring—something unspoken, a spark that hadn't been there before, or maybe he'd just never let himself see it. He swallowed hard, the café's warmth fading as a chill crept in, her words echoing—*choose different*—and he sensed a fracture forming, a crack in the life he'd clung to.

"There's more," Juno said, her voice dropping low, an edge cutting through, sharp as the neon outside. "Something you need to know—something big."

He leaned in, pulse quickening, sensing the gravity in her tone. "What?"

She hesitated, eyes flicking to the café's shadowed corners, then back, her voice barely above a whisper. "Project Sentinel," she said, the words heavy, deliberate. "It's not just another surveillance grid—it's worse, Lukas. A system to predict dissent, flag people before they even think of rebelling. No trials, no proof—just detention, erasure, based on algorithms. It's live soon, and your father's driving it."

His stomach dropped, the coffee turning sour in his throat, Juno's words sinking like lead—*predict dissent, detention*—and he gripped the mug tighter, knuckles white. "How do you know this?" he asked, voice low and tight, eyes searching hers for any crack, any doubt.

Her gaze hardened, a flicker of defiance sparking. "Resistance," she said, voice steady but fierce, leaning closer, her hand tightening faint on his. "I've seen plans, heard whispers—hacked Ministry feeds, scraps from defectors. It's moving fast—faster than we can counter. And Baron—he's not just involved, he's the damn architect."

Lukas's chest tightened, his breath shallow, but he kept his face stone, though his mind raced—*of course he is, always is*—Baron's shadow stretching long, inescapable. "What are you asking?" he said, voice tight, leaning back a hair, the mug cold in his hands. "Sabotage it? Join your fight?"

Juno's expression softened, but her eyes held fire, unyielding. "I'm asking you to see it," she said, voice low and urgent, her hand still on his, warm and firm. "You're in deep—Council access, data streams, his trust. You could slow it, Lukas, give us a shot to stop it. Or you can keep blind, let Sentinel crush anyone who dares think free—me, the Slums, maybe you one day."

He sat back, the weight of her words crashing heavy, Juno's hand falling away slow, leaving a chill where it'd been—

crush anyone, me—and the café's hum faded, rain drumming louder, a pulse that matched the storm in his chest. He'd known his father's reach was vast, but this—predictive detention, lives snuffed on a guess—was a line he hadn't seen coming, a truth that cracked the world he'd known.

"I can't just…" Lukas started, voice low, trailing off, shaking his head slow. "Betray him, the Council—it's all I've got, Juno. If I burn that, what's left? Who am I without it?"

Her eyes held his, sad but fierce, unyielding. "Someone who chose," she said, voice quiet but sharp, cutting deep. "Someone who fought, not followed. You're more than his shadow, Lukas—you've just never let yourself see it."

The Council's central building gleamed sterile under dawn's gray light, its glass walls reflecting the Upper City's spires like a mirror to Neo Haven's cold ambition. Lukas sat at his desk in the analyst wing, the hum of monitors and soft tapping of keyboards a dull drone around him, his holo-interface flickering with data streams—economic trends, social patterns, dissent metrics—all feeding the Council's grip. His eyes scanned the projections, but his mind churned, Juno's words from the café clawing relentless—*Project Sentinel, predict dissent, crush it*—and the weight of them pressed hard, a vise tightening around his thoughts.

He'd always brushed off Juno's hints about the Council's darker edges—surveillance, control, the All-Seeing Eye—but her tone last night had cut deeper, raw and urgent, and now doubt gnawed, a splinter he couldn't ignore. *Sentinel*—a name he'd never heard, but it burned in his gut, and as his fingers danced across the interface, pulling up routine reports, a file name snagged his eye—*Sentinel01_confidential*—buried in a subfolder, innocuous but glaring now, like a trap waiting to spring.

His heart skipped, pulse ticking fast, and he glanced around—analysts hunched at their stations, faces lit by holo-glow, oblivious, the office calm but heavy with the Council's ever-present watch. He hesitated, fingers hovering over the controls, the air suddenly cold—*if I open this, no going back*—but Juno's voice echoed, *"You're in a position to stop it"*, and he swiped the file open, breath hitching as data flooded the screen.

At first, it read like any surveillance report—metrics, grids, risk vectors—familiar, mundane. Then it shifted, lines of code peeling back to reveal something darker: *Predictive Models: Dissent Likelihood, Detainment Protocols, Preemptive Neutralization.* Lukas's eyes scanned fast, the words sinking like stones—Sentinel wasn't just monitoring, it was *preempting*, flagging citizens not for crimes but for *potential*, tracking every move, word, transaction, feeding it into algorithms that spit out threat scores. A flagged score meant detention—no trial, no appeal, just erasure, lives snuffed on a machine's guess. Names scrolled—*Juno Varek, Risk Factor 87%*—and his stomach dropped, her face flashing in his mind, fierce and steady, now a number in Sentinel's crosshairs.

He closed the file fast, heart pounding loud in his ears, the office's hum fading to a dull roar. *This is what he's building*—

Baron, the architect, not just controlling but crushing, stripping humanity for order. Lukas's fists clenched tight, nails biting his palms, the weight of it crashing—*not just Juno, anyone, everyone*—and he couldn't unsee it, couldn't unknow the cage his father was forging.

He shoved back from the desk, chair scraping shrill, and moved fast, legs carrying him through the building's sterile corridors—glass walls gleaming, drones buzzing soft in the distance—toward the private wing, Baron's office, a fortress of steel and power. He didn't knock, bursting through the door, breath ragged, finding his father behind a massive desk, holo-displays floating around him like a crown of data, his sharp gray eyes flicking up, surprise flashing brief before hardening to stone.

"Lukas," Baron said, voice cool and measured, rising slow, hands clasped behind his back. "What's this about?"

Lukas stepped forward, chest tight, words spilling fierce. "I know about Sentinel," he said, voice low and raw, trembling with the weight of it. "Predicting dissent, locking people up—innocents—on a guess. How could you let this happen?"

Baron's expression faltered, a flicker of shock crossing his face, gone fast as his jaw set, eyes narrowing cold. "I see," he said, voice clipped, stepping around the desk, his shadow falling long across the polished floor. "You've been digging where you don't belong."

"How could you?" Lukas pressed, voice rising, sharp with disbelief, stepping closer, hands clenched tight. "You're talking about lives—people like Juno, like anyone who dares think for themselves. It's wrong, Father, it's tyranny."

Baron's gaze sharpened, his voice dropping to a dangerous edge, cold as the steel walls. "You don't understand the burden we carry, Lukas," he said, stepping forward, looming tall. "Neo Haven survives because we control it—because I control it. Sentinel's necessary—dissent festers, chaos waits, and we can't afford to react. We preempt, we protect, we keep this city from falling apart."

"Protect?" Lukas echoed, voice cracking, anger flaring hot in his chest, stepping into his father's space, rain drumming loud outside the window, mirroring the storm inside. "You're crushing them—locking up innocents, predicting crimes that haven't happened. That's not protection, it's fear—your fear, not theirs."

Baron's face twisted, rage breaking through his calm, and he leaned in close, voice a low snarl. "You're naive, boy," he said, words cutting sharp. "You think those Slums rats wouldn't burn this city down if we let them? You think your little friend—Juno—wouldn't slit our throats for her precious freedom? Sentinel's the shield, the hard choice—my choice—to keep us strong."

Lukas shook his head, throat tight, the words a gut-punch—*Juno, a threat*—and he stepped back, voice trembling but fierce. "You're wrong," he said, low and steady, eyes burning into his father's. "You're not shielding—you're strangling. I won't be part of it, not this—not you."

Baron's eyes flashed, fury and betrayal mingling, and his voice dropped to a deadly whisper, colder than the rain. "Then you're weak," he said, stepping closer, towering. "Always were—too soft, too sentimental. I molded you, pushed you, for this city, for our name. But you're no Tellar—you're nothing."

The words hit like a blade, slicing deep, and Lukas felt his chest cave, the ache of his father's contempt a wound he'd always feared. But something shifted—anger, resolve, a spark he hadn't known he had—and he straightened, jaw clenched tight, voice steady despite the storm inside. "I'm not you," he said, low and final, stepping back, the rain's drum a roar now. "I never was—I'm done being your shadow."

Baron's face froze, rage hardening to stone, and he turned away, back to the window, voice flat and final. "Get out," he said, not looking back. "You're no son of mine—not anymore."

Lukas didn't flinch, the words a blow but freeing, a chain snapping loose, and he turned sharp, walking out, the door's thud behind him echoing final in the sterile hall. The pain burned, raw and deep, but beneath it—relief, a strange lightness. He'd crossed the line, burned the Tellar name, and for the first time, he felt the weight lift, his steps carrying him not toward Baron's cage but somewhere new, undefined, his own.

The Council's central building gleamed sterile under dawn's gray light, its glass walls reflecting the Upper City's spires like a mirror to Neo Haven's cold ambition. Lukas sat at his desk in the analyst wing, the hum of monitors and soft tapping of keyboards a dull drone around him, his holo-interface flickering with data streams—economic trends, social patterns, dissent metrics—all feeding the Council's grip. His eyes scanned the projections, but his mind churned, Juno's words from the café clawing relentless—*Project Sentinel, predict dissent, crush it*—and the weight of them pressed hard, a vise tightening around his thoughts.

He'd always brushed off Juno's hints about the Council's darker edges—surveillance, control, the All-Seeing Eye—but her tone last night had cut deeper, raw and urgent, and now doubt gnawed, a splinter he couldn't ignore. *Sentinel*—a name he'd never heard, but it burned in his gut, and as his fingers danced across the interface, pulling up routine reports, a file name snagged his eye—*Sentinel01_confidential*—buried in a subfolder, innocuous but glaring now, like a trap waiting to spring.

His heart skipped, pulse ticking fast, and he glanced around—analysts hunched at their stations, faces lit by holo-glow, oblivious, the office calm but heavy with the Council's ever-present watch. He hesitated, fingers hovering over the controls, the air suddenly cold—*if I open this, no going back*—but Juno's voice echoed, *"You're in a position to stop it"*, and he swiped the file open, breath hitching as data flooded the screen.

At first, it read like any surveillance report—metrics, grids, risk vectors—familiar, mundane. Then it shifted, lines of code peeling back to reveal something darker: *Predictive Models: Dissent Likelihood, Detainment Protocols, Preemptive Neutralization.* Lukas's eyes scanned fast, the words sinking like stones— Sentinel wasn't just monitoring, it was *preempting*, flagging citizens not for crimes but for *potential*, tracking every move, word, transaction, feeding it into algorithms that spit out threat scores. A flagged score meant detention—no trial, no appeal, just erasure, lives snuffed on a machine's guess. Names scrolled—*Juno Varek, Risk Factor 87%*—and his stomach dropped, her face flashing in his mind, fierce and steady, now a number in Sentinel's crosshairs.

He closed the file fast, heart pounding loud in his ears, the office's hum fading to a dull roar. *This is what he's building*— Baron, the architect, not just controlling but crushing, stripping humanity for order. Lukas's fists clenched tight, nails biting his palms, the weight of it crashing—*not just Juno, anyone, everyone*— and he couldn't unsee it, couldn't unknow the cage his father was forging.

He shoved back from the desk, chair scraping shrill, and moved fast, legs carrying him through the building's sterile corridors—glass walls gleaming, drones buzzing soft in the distance—toward the private wing, Baron's office, a fortress of steel and power. He didn't knock, bursting through the door, breath ragged, finding his father behind a massive desk, holo-displays floating around him like a crown of data, his sharp gray eyes flicking up, surprise flashing brief before hardening to stone.

"Lukas," Baron said, voice cool and measured, rising slow, hands clasped behind his back. "What's this about?"

Lukas stepped forward, chest tight, words spilling fierce. "I know about Sentinel," he said, voice low and raw, trembling with the weight of it. "Predicting dissent, locking people up—innocents—on a guess. How could you let this happen?"

Baron's expression faltered, a flicker of shock crossing his face, gone fast as his jaw set, eyes narrowing cold. "I see," he said, voice clipped, stepping around the desk, his shadow falling long across the polished floor. "You've been digging where you don't belong."

"How could you?" Lukas pressed, voice rising, sharp with disbelief, stepping closer, hands clenched tight. "You're talking about lives—people like Juno, like anyone who dares think for themselves. It's wrong, Father, it's tyranny."

Baron's gaze sharpened, his voice dropping to a dangerous edge, cold as the steel walls. "You don't understand the burden we carry, Lukas," he said, stepping forward, looming tall. "Neo Haven survives because we control it— because I control it. Sentinel's necessary—dissent festers, chaos waits, and we can't afford to react. We preempt, we protect, we keep this city from falling apart."

"Protect?" Lukas echoed, voice cracking, anger flaring hot in his chest, stepping into his father's space, rain drumming loud outside the window, mirroring the storm inside. "You're crushing them—locking up innocents, predicting crimes that haven't happened. That's not protection, it's fear—your fear, not theirs."

Baron's face twisted, rage breaking through his calm, and he leaned in close, voice a low snarl. "You're naive, boy," he said, words cutting sharp. "You think those Slums rats wouldn't burn this city down if we let them? You think your little friend—Juno—wouldn't slit our throats for her precious freedom? Sentinel's the shield, the hard choice—my choice—to keep us strong."

Lukas shook his head, throat tight, the words a gut-punch—*Juno, a threat*—and he stepped back, voice trembling but fierce. "You're wrong," he said, low and steady, eyes burning into his father's. "You're not shielding—you're strangling. I won't be part of it, not this—not you."

Baron's eyes flashed, fury and betrayal mingling, and his voice dropped to a deadly whisper, colder than the rain. "Then you're weak," he said, stepping closer, towering. "Always were—too soft, too sentimental. I molded you, pushed you, for this city, for our name. But you're no Tellar—you're nothing."

The words hit like a blade, slicing deep, and Lukas felt his chest cave, the ache of his father's contempt a wound he'd always feared. But something shifted—anger, resolve, a spark he hadn't known he had—and he straightened, jaw clenched tight, voice steady despite the storm inside. "I'm not you," he said, low and final, stepping back, the rain's drum a roar now. "I never was—I'm done being your shadow."

Baron's face froze, rage hardening to stone, and he turned away, back to the window, voice flat and final. "Get out," he said, not looking back. "You're no son of mine—not anymore."

Lukas didn't flinch, the words a blow but freeing, a chain snapping loose, and he turned sharp, walking out, the door's thud behind him echoing final in the sterile hall. The pain burned, raw and deep, but beneath it—relief, a strange lightness. He'd crossed the line, burned the Tellar name, and for the first time, he felt the weight lift, his steps carrying him not toward Baron's cage but somewhere new, undefined, his own.

Lukas paced a shadowed alley in the Old City, neon flickering weak above—pink, green, their buzz drowned by the rain's steady patter, the air thick with ash and the faint tang of rad-dust from the '52 meltdown zones nearby. His thoughts churned, a storm of Baron's dismissal—*"You're nothing"*—and Juno's plea—*"You can stop this"*—clashing wild, each step heavier, the weight of his choice sinking deep. He'd walked away, severed ties, but the fracture lines in his life—identity, purpose—gaped wider, and fear gnawed, sharp and cold: *What now? Who am I without him?*

Juno slipped from the shadows, quiet as a blade, her leather jacket slick with rain, her dark eyes catching his with that piercing intensity—seeing him, not the Tellar heir, but Lukas, raw and unmoored. "You look like death warmed over," she said, voice soft but edged, stepping close, her boots scuffing wet gravel, a faint smirk tugging her lips despite the concern flickering in her gaze.

He gave a weak half-smile, rain dripping from his hair, soaking his shirt, the cold grounding but not enough to quiet the chaos inside. "Feel it," he muttered, voice low and rough, leaning against the alley's rusted wall, the metal cold through his jacket. "Did it—told Baron everything. Sentinel, the truth—he's done with me. Disowned me, right there."

Juno's eyes widened a fraction, softening fast, and she stepped closer, her hand brushing his arm light, a warmth that cut through the rain's chill. "Damn, Lukas," she said, voice quiet, heavy with the weight of it, her fingers lingering a beat, steadying him. "That's… I know what that cost you. I'm sorry."

He shook his head, rain streaking his face, the ache still raw but lighter somehow, Juno's touch a tether. "Don't be," he said, voice steadier now, meeting her gaze, dark and fierce. "Had to—Sentinel's wrong, he's wrong. Couldn't stay blind, not after what you said. The leak—did it hit?"

Her smirk returned, sharp and bright, and she nodded quick, pulling him toward a low doorway tucked in the alley's shadow, its neon sign—*"Undergrid"*—flickering faint. "Hit hard," she said, voice lifting with a spark of hope, pushing the door open, the creak loud in the quiet. "Come see."

Inside, the resistance hub hummed—a cramped basement, walls patched with steel and graffiti, holo-screens flickering green and blue, casting jagged light across a dozen figures—Slums hackers, ex-Ministry runners, faces gaunt but eyes fierce, their murmurs a low buzz of defiance. Juno led him to a screen bank, data streaming fast—*Sentinel disrupted, Council delays, resistance spikes*—and Lukas stared, the scope hitting him: his leak, Juno's channel, had cracked the city's armor, stirred its pulse.

"More joining daily," Juno said, tapping a screen, her voice fierce now, laced with resolve. "Your files—proof of Sentinel's reach, its detentions—lit a fire. Slums are waking, Old City's buzzing, even Upper City whispers. We're slowing it, Lukas—maybe stopping it."

He nodded slow, the screens' glow reflecting in his eyes, a strange lightness blooming—*I did this*—but the weight lingered, Baron's voice—*"Weak…"*—and the fracture lines in his identity, still raw. "I'm not sure what I am now," he admitted, voice quiet, glancing at her, Juno's face steady, fierce. "Walked away—but what's left? No name, no place."

She stepped close, hand on his arm again, firm and warm, her voice soft but unyielding. "You're you," she said, eyes locking his, dark and piercing. "Not his shadow, not a Tellar—just Lukas, choosing to fight. That's enough—it's more than enough."

He held her gaze, the rain's drum fading, her words a spark—*just Lukas*—and for the first time, he felt it, a path forming, rough but his. The fight wasn't over—Sentinel loomed, the Council's grip tightened—but he'd chosen, stepped free, and as Juno's hand lingered, their bond a quiet fire, he knew he'd face it on his terms, no one else's.

THE LAST PREDICTION

A Neo Haven Short Story, 2143 AD

sabel Raine's fingers hovered over the holographic interface, her eyes skimming the endless streams of data pouring in from the Ministry of Predictive Justice's vast surveillance networks. She had done this every day for five years now, watching, categorizing, and flagging anomalies. Each line of code, each fragment of human behavior tracked by drones, street cameras, and biometrics, was analyzed and fed into the Ministry's predictive algorithms.

Above her, the sleek, gray walls of the Ministry's data hub pulsed faintly with the hum of endless computation. It was a far cry from the world outside. The streets of Neo Haven, drenched in rain and neon lights, were chaotic, filled with people who went about their daily lives under the invisible gaze of the Ministry. They didn't understand how things worked behind these walls. They didn't need to. Order was kept, and that was all that mattered.

Isabel was a small cog in this vast machine, just another analyst processing terabytes of human activity, ensuring that the city remained safe from chaos. She wore the same blank expression as the others in her row; hundreds of analysts like her, each locked in their own pod, their minds tethered to the algorithm that maintained peace. The work was precise and monotonous, but it was important. At least, that's what she had convinced herself.

The sound of soft rain was tapping against the reinforced windows of the hub, a soothing rhythm in the otherwise sterile space. Her shift was almost over. She'd flagged twelve potential threats today—small-time infractions, petty theft, low-level conspiracy murmurs in the outer districts. Each had been handed over to Enforcement for preemptive arrest.

Routine.

Isabel blinked, her eyes tired from staring at the constant stream of predictive readouts. She tapped a few commands into the console, her hand wavering slightly as the fatigue of the day set in. Just a few more reports to file and she could go home.

Then, the screen flickered red.

Anomaly detected.

The warning flashed across her screen, cold and mechanical. Isabel's fingers flew over the keyboard as she pulled up the report. Her breath caught in her throat. The anomaly wasn't just a minor statistical blip. It was a full predictive alert—a high-level alert that the system rarely, if ever, flagged.

She felt a cold sweat break out across her skin. The Ministry's predictive algorithms had calculated something big. Something dangerous.

A rebellion.

Isabel's pulse quickened as the details began to fill the screen. The data was patchy, incomplete, but the conclusions were terrifyingly clear. A major uprising was imminent. The algorithm had detected signs of civil unrest, hidden beneath layers of innocuous behavior, carefully buried under the surface of society. The system had pulled from hundreds of thousands of surveillance feeds, monitoring everything from conversations in dingy bars to patterns of credit transactions in the city's underbelly.

She watched in stunned silence as the details emerged: planned attacks, the spread of propaganda, coded messages traveling across secure lines. The predictive system had pieced it all together into a coherent narrative.

But it was the final line that made her blood run cold.

Predicted instigator: Isabel Raine.

Her hands stopped moving, hovering inches above the console as the world around her seemed to freeze. The text blinked back at her, mocking her with its certainty. She stared at her own name, her breath shallow and uneven. This had to be a mistake. There was no way—*no way*—the system could be predicting her involvement. She wasn't a revolutionary. She wasn't part of any underground movement. She was just a data analyst. A nobody.

She swallowed hard, her mouth dry. This couldn't be happening.

Isabel forced herself to move, quickly closing the report and pulling up the system logs. There had to be an explanation. A glitch in the system. A corrupted data set that linked her name to this mess by mistake. She could fix this. She just had to find the source of the error.

Her fingers trembled as she dug deeper into the data, cross-referencing every thread the system had followed to arrive at its conclusion. The algorithm was cold, logical, dispassionate. It followed patterns and probabilities, drawing from mountains of data to make its predictions. There was no room for error.

She scrolled through the surveillance logs, her eyes scanning the timestamps and metadata. Conversations in bars, encrypted messages on back channels, even stray words spoken in passing-by people she didn't know. But the threads connected back to her.

"Isabel Raine will be responsible for a violent uprising in Neo Haven."

Her stomach turned. The system wasn't wrong. It rarely was. That was the point of the Ministry, after all. To prevent crime, not react to it. To predict rebellion before it could happen. And now it had predicted her.

The weight of it pressed down on her, suffocating. She knew how this worked. She had processed hundreds of cases like this before, had seen the files passed to Enforcement, had seen the quiet disappearances of those flagged by the system.

Once your name was in the database, it was over. The algorithm determined your fate. There was no trial, no appeal. No way out.

Her thoughts raced, a storm of panic and disbelief. What had she done? What had she said? She racked her brain, trying to remember any moment where she might have slipped, where her words or actions could have been misconstrued as rebellious. But she found nothing. She had lived her life in compliance, kept her head down, and followed the rules.

Her breath came in shallow gasps. She glanced around the room, suddenly hyper-aware of the dozens of other analysts, each glued to their own screens, completely unaware of the catastrophe unfolding in her world. She was alone.

The air felt heavy, oppressive. Isabel could feel the cold gaze of the Ministry's surveillance system on her, the same gaze that had been turned outward on the city for years, now focused squarely on her. There was no escape from it. The walls seemed to close in, the sterile lights overhead casting long, sharp shadows.

Her hands moved on instinct, closing down the anomaly report, wiping any trace of her access from the logs. She couldn't let this get out. Not yet. Not until she figured out what to do.

A single thought gripped her with terrifying clarity: *Run.*

But where? There was nowhere in Neo Haven that the Ministry's eyes didn't reach, no corner of the city that wasn't under constant surveillance. She had seen the predictive algorithms at work. They could track patterns in movement, in behavior, could predict when and where someone might flee long before they made the decision themselves.

If she ran, it would confirm everything. The system would mark her as a threat, and she would be hunted down, preemptively erased before the rebellion could even begin.

But if she stayed, if she did nothing… *was the uprising inevitable?*

Her mind spiraled. Had the prediction been made because of something she hadn't even done yet? Or had seeing the prediction itself set the events in motion? Was she destined to lead this rebellion because the system had said she would?

The lines between cause and effect blurred in her mind, tangled in a knot of paranoia and fear. If the system had already predicted it, did she even have a choice?

She clenched her fists, her nails digging into her palms. The pain grounded her, but only for a moment. There was no way to think clearly now. Her entire world had been turned upside down in the space of minutes. The system had branded her as a future criminal, a leader of a revolution that hadn't even happened yet.

But if there was one thing Isabel figured, it was that the system couldn't be perfect. She'd seen the cracks before, the small inconsistencies, the occasional errors that got swept under the rug to maintain the illusion of infallibility. And now, she had to find a way to exploit those cracks.

She turned sharply from her pod and walked quickly across the room, trying to act casual, though her heart raced in her chest. Analysts around her sat at their own terminals, typing away, reviewing predictive reports with blank expressions. None of them looked up. She passed rows and rows of data streams, each pod identical to the last, until she reached the exit.

Isabel took a deep breath and stepped outside into the sterile, brightly lit hallways of the Ministry. The walls were cold steel, illuminated by the pale glow of overhead lights. The sound of her footsteps echoed sharply as she hurried down the corridor, the rhythm of her boots against the tile floor unnerving. She could hear her heartbeat pounding in her ears.

Every corner she turned, she half-expected Enforcement agents to appear, their faceless visors locking onto her, hands on their pulse rifles, waiting to drag her away. It was only a matter of time before the system flagged her. That's what it did. It watched, and it waited. The entire Ministry was a machine designed to preempt human rebellion. And she was at its mercy.

Keep walking. The words felt hollow, like an order from some distant part of her mind. Her legs moved stiffly, as if disconnected from her body. She turned another corner, heading toward the lower levels. There was someone she needed to see.

By the time she reached Unit 7, a secluded part of the Ministry reserved for only the most classified data analysts, Isabel's skin prickled with the ever-present weight of surveillance. The Ministry's security network hung over her like a fog; drones patrolling the upper levels, biometric scanners installed at every checkpoint, AI monitoring the flow of personnel in real-time. But Unit 7 was different. It was where the real work happened. The people in this unit dealt with things that never saw the light of day.

And deep down, Isabel knew Gareth Quinlan could help her.

Gareth wasn't just a colleague she'd worked with occasionally. He was the closest thing Isabel had to a friend in the Ministry—a mentor, even. When she had first been assigned to the Predictive Justice team five years ago, it was Gareth who had taken her under his wing. He'd been the one to show her how the algorithms worked, how to navigate the endless sea of data, how to see through the façade of perfect justice that the Ministry maintained. He had hinted, in quiet conversations late at night, that not everything in the system was as flawless as it seemed.

More than once, he had covered for her when she made mistakes in the early days. She owed him for that. But more importantly, she trusted him.

The door to Unit 7 slid open with a soft hiss, revealing a narrow hallway lined with sleek white walls. At the far end stood a single door, sealed and unmarked. Isabel's wrist-pad buzzed softly as she passed through the biometric scanners, and she hesitated, glancing down to see her own identification code flash across the small screen embedded in her skin.

Do they know I'm here?

The thought sent a wave of nausea through her. The Ministry's algorithms could track every movement, every decision, and flag anomalies almost instantly. Her arrival at Unit 7 might already be raising questions. She forced herself to keep walking, her feet carrying her to the unmarked door at the end of the hall.

Behind it was Gareth Quinlan: anomaly detection specialist, but also one of the few people left in Neo Haven who still believed in something beyond the system. He had never explicitly said it, but over the years, Isabel had come to sense that Gareth was one of the few people who saw through the Ministry's control. He never spoke about it openly, but there were times when his cynicism toward the predictive models slipped through, like cracks in an otherwise impenetrable wall.

The door slid open silently, revealing a dimly lit room cluttered with monitors and tangled wires. The faint glow of data streams flickered in the low light. Gareth sat hunched over a console, his back to her, engrossed in the lines of code cascading down his screen. His fingers moved rapidly over the interface, a blur of motion as he input command after command.

"Gareth?" Isabel's voice was quiet, almost a whisper, but it echoed unnervingly in the small room.

He didn't turn around. "Busy."

"I need your help," she said, stepping into the room, her voice shaking despite her best efforts to stay calm. "It's important."

Gareth paused for a moment, his fingers hovering over the keys. Slowly, he turned to face her, his sharp eyes narrowing as he took in her pale face and trembling hands. His expression softened, though his usual guardedness remained. "Isabel, what's going on? You're not supposed to be here."

Isabel could feel her chest tighten, her throat dry. "Gareth... I think I've been flagged."

There was a long, heavy silence. Gareth's eyes flickered with something, concern, perhaps. But it was quickly buried under a mask of neutrality. He gestured for her to sit. "Tell me everything."

Isabel quickly recounted what had happened; the strange flicker on her screen, the report of the rebellion, and how her own name had appeared as the instigator. As she spoke, her voice wavered, her fear evident in every word. Gareth listened quietly, his face unreadable, though his eyes occasionally darted to the console behind him, as if already calculating the risk of their conversation.

When she finished, Gareth sighed, running a hand through his graying hair. He leaned back in his chair, folding his arms across his chest. "You weren't supposed to see that."

"I know," Isabel replied, her voice barely above a whisper. "But it's there, Gareth. The system thinks I'm going to lead a rebellion. It's already flagged me. What do I do?"

Gareth stared at her for a moment, his eyes narrowing slightly, as if he was weighing his next words carefully. "The system doesn't make mistakes, Isabel. Not in the way you're hoping."

Isabel's heart sank. "So that's it, then? I'm done for?"

Gareth shook his head. "Not necessarily. But you need to understand something. The predictive algorithms…they don't determine reality. They identify patterns, behaviors— potential threats. It's designed to be *precise,* but it's still just an algorithm. And sometimes, it sees potential where it shouldn't."

Isabel frowned. "So, it's wrong?"

Gareth's eyes softened. "Not wrong, but incomplete. It's reacting to the data it's given, and sometimes, when all the signs are there, it flags someone. It is not predicting your fate. It's predicting potential. It doesn't mean you're going to lead a rebellion. But now… now the system thinks you might. That's enough to put you on their radar."

The words hit her like a punch to the gut. "But I haven't done anything. I've never broken the law, never even thought about…"

She trailed off, the reality settling over her. It didn't matter what she *hadn't* done. The system saw a pattern, and now she was a potential threat. That was enough.

"I've seen this happen before," Gareth said quietly. "It's rare, but it happens. The algorithm is good, but it's not perfect. It sees patterns where there may be none. The worst part is, once you're flagged, it's hard to shake."

Her heart pounded in her chest. "So, what do I do? How do I fix this?"

Gareth glanced at his console, then back at her. His expression was grave. "There's not much you can do. The system will keep an eye on you now. You'll be monitored; every move, every interaction. And the more they watch, the more likely it is they'll find something. It becomes a cycle. That's how it works. It doesn't mean you're guilty, but…"

"But I'll look guilty," Isabel finished, her voice barely above a whisper.

Gareth nodded. "Exactly."

A cold chill ran down Isabel's spine. Now that it had flagged her, every action she took could be seen through that lens. The fear was starting to close in, tightening around her chest. She couldn't breathe.

"I can't stay here," she said, her voice shaking. "If I stay, they'll find something. They'll make me into the person they think I'm going to be."

Gareth leaned back in his chair, his face drawn. "Running is dangerous. The system tracks everything, and once they know you've gone rogue, it'll confirm their suspicions. You'll be hunted."

Her hands trembled, her mind racing. She didn't have a choice. "What would you do?"

Gareth's eyes softened, and for a moment, she saw the weariness in him, the years of working inside a system that saw everything but understood nothing. "I'd run," he said softly. "It's the only way you might stand a chance."

The words hung heavy in the air, the weight of them sinking into Isabel's bones. She looked at Gareth, the man who had guided her through the labyrinth of data and predictions, the man she trusted more than anyone else in this godforsaken place. She had always known the system wasn't perfect, that it had cracks. But now, she was caught in one of those cracks, and the only way out was to disappear.

"Why are you helping me?" she asked, her voice small.

Gareth gave her a sad smile. "Because I've seen too many people go through this. People who didn't deserve it. You're one of the good ones, Isabel. You don't deserve to be chewed up by this machine."

Her throat tightened, and she nodded, her heart heavy with gratitude and fear. "Thank you."

Gareth reached into his desk and pulled out a small data chip. "This will give you a head start. It'll mask your movements for a while, give you a window to get out before the system catches on. But it won't last long."

Isabel took the chip, her hands trembling. "Why do you—" she stops herself before finishing her question. Her eyes linger on him, a growing understanding growing between them. Then, "Where do I go?"

He shrugged. "Somewhere they can't reach. Off-grid. There are places in the city, underground networks that operate outside the Ministry's reach. But you'll have to be careful."

She nodded, slipping the chip into her wrist-pad. "I will."

Gareth leaned forward, his eyes locking onto hers. "Listen to me, Isabel. Once you're out, you can't come back. They'll mark you as a fugitive, and there'll be no second chances. You need to disappear completely."

Isabel swallowed hard, the weight of his words settling over her like a heavy blanket. "I understand."

With that, Gareth leaned back, a weary sigh escaping his lips. "Good luck."

As she turned to leave, her heart racing, Isabel knew this was the last time she would ever see him. She walked out of Unit 7, the halls of the Ministry cold and oppressive around her, and with every step, the realization sank deeper into her bones.

The system had flagged her. It had seen a future where she was a rebel, a threat to the order of Neo Haven.

And now, whether she liked it or not, that future was starting to take shape.

The frigid wind of Neo Haven's alleyways hit Isabel like a slap in the face, the scent of rain and city smoke swirling around her as she hurried through the narrow streets. Every step felt heavier than the last, her heartbeat thudding in her ears, drowning out the sound of distant drone patrols. She didn't belong here, in the shadows of the undercity, but there was nowhere else for her to go. Not now.

She had made it out of the Ministry unnoticed, at least for now; but she knew it wouldn't be long before the system flagged her absence. Even with Gareth's data chip masking her movements, it was only a matter of time before the predictive algorithms caught up. She didn't know how much time she had, but every second felt like a countdown.

I'm running. I'm actually running. The thought chilled her, sinking deeper into her gut with every breath. She had seen hundreds of people flagged by the system, their lives erased the moment they became "threats." And now, she was one of them; a name on a list, a statistic in a machine that cared nothing for intent, only probability.

The streets of the lower city were a labyrinth of tight corners, old alleyways, and rusted metal walkways. Neon signs flickered above her, casting garish light across the crumbling walls. People moved around her like ghosts, eyes down, their faces hidden beneath hoods and augmented visors. They didn't see her. If they did, they didn't care. The lower city was where people disappeared, where the Ministry's surveillance didn't reach as far. At least, that's what she had always heard.

She ducked into a side alley, pressing her back against the cool stone wall as she caught her breath. Her mind raced, the pressure building in her chest like a vice. The chip Gareth had given her was still running, hiding her movements from the Ministry's network, but it was only temporary. Once it ran out, she'd be exposed. She needed to figure out what to do next. Fast.

She thought of Gareth's words. *Underground networks that operate outside the Ministry's reach.* Places where people like her—people marked as potential threats—went to disappear. But even if she found one, would it be enough? The Ministry's reach was long, and its algorithms were relentless. How far could she really run before they caught up to her?

Isabel closed her eyes, leaning her head back against the wall. She had always believed in the system. Believed in its efficiency, its ability to keep order, to protect the city from chaos. But now, with her own life hanging in the balance, she couldn't shake the growing sense that the system was flawed—more than flawed. Dangerous.

She opened her eyes, staring up at the faint glow of the neon lights overhead. The rain had started again, a light drizzle that coated everything in a slick sheen. She could hear the distant hum of drones patrolling the upper levels, keeping watch over the city. Up there, life continued as usual, the illusion of peace and security maintained by the algorithms she had once trusted.

But down here, in the shadows, the truth was different.

Her wrist-pad buzzed softly, and she flinched, instinctively pulling back her sleeve to check the notification. For a moment, her heart leapt into her throat- had the Ministry already found her? But it was just a low- power warning. The chip Gareth had given her was running out of juice.

She needed to move.

Taking a deep breath, Isabel pushed herself off the wall and began walking again, her eyes scanning the maze of streets for any sign of the people Gareth had mentioned. She didn't know where to start, but she had heard rumors; stories about old subway tunnels deep beneath the city, places where the Ministry's surveillance didn't penetrate. If anyone could help her, it would be there.

As she moved deeper into the lower levels, the streets became darker, the shadows thicker. The people around her moved like phantoms, their faces obscured by hoods and masks, their bodies hunched against the rain. The sound of dripping water echoed off the walls, mixing with the low hum of machinery from the industrial zones nearby.

Isabel's chest tightened as she approached an old subway station, its entrance half-collapsed and covered in graffiti. The tunnels below were long-abandoned, left to rot after the city's higher levels were built. But she had heard whispers that the underground was still inhabited by those who couldn't afford to live above ground, or by those who wanted to disappear.

She hesitated at the entrance, her heart racing. This was it. Her last chance.

Taking a deep breath, she stepped inside.

The tunnels were dark, the air thick with the smell of mildew and rust. Water dripped from the ceiling, pooling in shallow puddles along the cracked concrete floor. Isabel moved carefully, her footsteps echoing in the silence. The deeper she went, the more oppressive the darkness became, closing in around her like a suffocating blanket.

She had no idea where she was going, but she kept walking, following the faint signs of life she could hear in the distance- muffled voices, the occasional clatter of metal. As she rounded a corner, she spotted a faint light ahead, flickering dimly in the gloom.

Her heart pounded in her chest as she approached, her fingers brushing the edge of her wrist-pad, ready to send out a distress signal if things went south. But she knew that would be a last resort. The Ministry would come for her then, and there would be no escape.

As she drew closer, the light resolved into a makeshift camp; dozens of people huddled around small fires, their faces gaunt and tired. Some were wrapped in tattered blankets, others sat on crates, talking quietly among themselves. They were the forgotten, the people who had slipped through the cracks of Neo Haven's perfect system.

Isabel stepped forward cautiously, her eyes scanning the faces around her. They were all strangers, but they looked at her with a mixture of curiosity and wariness. She didn't belong here, but she needed their help.

"Looking for something?" a voice called from the shadows.

Isabel turned sharply, her heart skipping a beat. A man stepped out from the darkness, his face partially hidden beneath a hood. His eyes glinted in the firelight, sharp and calculating.

"I… I need to find someone," Isabel stammered, her voice shaky. "Someone who can help me disappear."

The man's lips curled into a small, humorless smile. "You're not the first. And you won't be the last."

Isabel swallowed hard, glancing around at the people gathered in the camp. "Do you know where I can find them?"

The man's gaze lingered on her for a moment before he nodded toward a tunnel leading deeper into the underground. "Keep walking. You'll find them if they want to be found."

Isabel hesitated, her stomach twisting with nerves. She didn't have a choice. She thanked the man quietly and continued down the tunnel, her footsteps echoing softly in the dark.

The air grew colder as she descended deeper into the underground, the light from the camp fading behind her. The tunnel seemed to stretch on forever, twisting and turning in ways that made her lose her sense of direction. Her heart pounded in her chest, and she felt a growing sense of unease creeping over her.

And then, she saw it: a figure standing at the far end of the tunnel, cloaked in shadows. Her breath caught in her throat as she approached cautiously, the figure remaining still, waiting for her.

"Isabel Raine," the figure said, their voice low and calm. "We've been expecting you."

Isabel's blood ran cold. "How do you know who I am?"

The figure stepped forward, the dim light illuminating their face; an older woman, her eyes sharp and calculating, yet there was a weariness in her expression. "The system flagged you, didn't it? You're one of us now."

Isabel's chest tightened. "One of you?"

The woman nodded, her gaze piercing. "You're a threat. At least, that's what they think. You've been marked. And now, you'll need to make a choice."

"What choice?" Isabel asked, her voice barely above a whisper.

The woman's eyes gleamed in the dim light. "You can run, like some of the others. Hide in the shadows, disappear from the system. Or…" She paused, her expression hardening. "You can fight."

Isabel's mind reeled. Fight? Against the system? Against everything she had been raised to believe in? The thought seemed impossible. But deep down, the fear that had been gnawing at her for days was starting to give way to something else.

Anger.

"They'll never stop," the woman said quietly. "Once you're marked, you're always a target. You can hide for a while, but they'll find you eventually. And when they do, you'll wish you had fought."

Isabel's hands clenched into fists at her sides. The system had branded her a rebel, a future criminal- someone to be erased. And now, she was starting to believe it. But she wasn't a threat. She wasn't a criminal. She was just someone trying to survive.

But maybe survival wasn't enough anymore.

Isabel met the woman's gaze, her voice steady. "Tell me what I need to do."

The woman's eyes flashed in the dim light of the tunnel, a knowing glint that sent a shiver down Isabel's spine. Her decision felt like a weight, pressing down on her chest, but the anger simmering beneath the surface drove her forward. She had been pushed too far, marked as something she wasn't. If the system believed she was a threat, then maybe it was time to become one.

The woman stepped closer, her voice quiet but firm. "You've chosen to fight. That's the first step. But the real question is, how far are you willing to go?"

Isabel swallowed hard, her mind still racing. "What do you mean?"

The woman regarded her carefully, as if weighing her words. "The system is vast, Isabel. It sees everything, controls everything. If you're serious about bringing it down, you have to understand that this isn't just about survival anymore. It's about dismantling the very thing that holds Neo Haven together."

Isabel's breath caught in her throat. Dismantle the system? The very thought seemed impossible. The Ministry of Predictive Justice wasn't just a building or a collection of servers. It was the bedrock of the city, the invisible force that kept everything in order, the one thing that people relied on for security.

But that security came at a cost. People like her—those who had been flagged by the system—were branded as threats before they even had the chance to prove otherwise.

The woman's voice cut through her thoughts. "We can't bring it down from the outside. We've tried. What we need is someone inside, someone who understands how the system works. Someone like you."

Isabel blinked, the realization hitting her hard. "You want me to… infiltrate the Ministry?"

The woman nodded. "You've worked there for years. You know the algorithms, the predictive models. You've seen how they flag people like us. We need that knowledge, Isabel. We need you."

Isabel hesitated, the enormity of what she was being asked to do sinking in. It wasn't just about running anymore. It was about fighting back, about using everything she knew to take down the very system she had once believed in. But the thought terrified her. If she went back into the Ministry, if she tried to sabotage the system from the inside, it would be a death sentence.

Her pulse quickened, her mind swirling with doubt. "And what happens if I get caught?"

The woman's face hardened. "You won't get caught. Not if we plan this right. But if you do… you know what the Ministry does to people like us. There's no coming back from that."

Isabel's stomach twisted. She had seen the disappearances, the quiet erasures of those who had been flagged by the system. No trials, no appeals. Just gone. And now she was standing at the edge of that same abyss, staring into the void, knowing that one wrong move could send her tumbling into it.

But what choice did she have? The system had already marked her for erasure. Running wouldn't save her. Hiding wouldn't change her fate. The only option left was to fight.

Her decision solidified, the fear giving way to determination. "What do I need to do?"

The woman's lips curled into a small, grim smile. "You're going to need allies. And you're going to need to gather as much intel as you can. The Ministry is vast, and it's guarded by some of the most advanced AI systems in the world. But there are weaknesses. There are always weaknesses."

Isabel nodded, her mind racing as she tried to piece together a plan. "Who do I talk to? Where do I start?"

The woman gestured for her to follow. "There's someone you need to meet. He's been with us for a long time, someone who knows the undercity inside and out. He'll help you find the people you need."

Isabel followed the woman deeper into the tunnels, the dim light flickering as they walked. Her heart pounded in her chest, every step feeling like a descent into the unknown. The underground seemed to stretch on forever, twisting and turning, until they reached a heavy metal door at the end of a long, narrow corridor.

The woman knocked once, and after a tense moment, the door creaked open. A man stood on the other side, his face obscured by the shadows. He stepped into the light, revealing a rugged face lined with age and experience. His eyes, though, were sharp; dangerously sharp, as if he missed nothing.

"This is Malik," the woman said, introducing him with a nod. "He's one of the leaders of the underground. He'll help you get what you need."

Malik's gaze flickered over Isabel, sizing her up. "You're the one who worked in the Ministry?"

Isabel nodded, her voice steady. "Yes."

He grunted, crossing his arms. "You don't look like much of a fighter."

"I don't have to be," she shot back, surprising herself with the edge in her voice. "I'm a data analyst. I know the system better than most on the outside."

Malik raised an eyebrow, then gave a slight nod of approval. "Good. We need someone with your skills. But you'd better be prepared for what's coming. Once you start down this path, there's no turning back."

"I understand," Isabel replied, her heart pounding. She was scared—more scared than she'd ever been in her life—but she couldn't show it. Not now. "What do I need to do?"

Malik glanced at the woman, then back at Isabel. "First, you'll need to prove yourself. There's a data terminal deeper in the underground, one the Ministry doesn't know about. It's old, buried beneath the city, but it still taps into the main network. We've been trying to get into it for months, but the security protocols are ancient. We need someone with your expertise to break through."

Isabel felt a surge of adrenaline. "I can do that."

Malik nodded. "Good. Once you're in, we'll be able to access some of the Ministry's older records—records that have been hidden away for years. We need that information if we're going to take down the system."

Isabel swallowed hard. "And after that?"

Malik's expression darkened. "After that, we take the fight to them."

- 216 -

ENDNOTES

<u>Dust, The Stoic Emperor:</u>

Marcus Aurelius, *Meditations*, Translated by Gregory Hays, Modern Library, 2003.
> Provides insight into Marcus Aurelius' Stoic philosophy and personal reflections on death and leadership.

Birley, Anthony R. *Marcus Aurelius: A Biography*. Routledge, 2000.
> A comprehensive biography covering Marcus Aurelius' life, reign, and the relationship with his son Commodus. Details the emperor's philosophical approach to leadership and his final military campaigns.

Cassius Dio, *Roman History*, Translated by Earnest Cary, Loeb Classical Library, Harvard University Press, 1914.
> Cassius Dio chronicles Marcus Aurelius' reign, including the military campaigns along the Danube and his final days. Dio also provides commentary on Commodus' early years as the heir to the empire.

Herodian, *History of the Roman Empire from the Death of Marcus Aurelius to the Accession of Gordian III*, Translated by C.R. Whittaker, Loeb Classical Library, Harvard University Press, 1969.
> Offers insight into the transition from Marcus Aurelius to Commodus, with detailed accounts of Marcus' death and the concerns surrounding Commodus' ascension to power.

The Augustan History: The Lives of the Later Caesars, Translated by Anthony Birley, Penguin Classics, 1976.
> A collection of Roman biographies that includes information on Marcus Aurelius' final campaign, his death, and the rise of Commodus. Although sometimes regarded as semi- historical, it remains an important source for this period.

Grant, Michael. *The Antonines: The Roman Empire in Transition*. Routledge, 1994.

> This text explores the reign of the Antonine emperors, including Marcus Aurelius' leadership during the Marcomannic Wars and the legacy he left to Commodus.

Le Bohec, Yann. *The Imperial Roman Army*. Routledge, 1994.

> Provides context for the Roman military during Marcus Aurelius' reign, particularly focusing on the structure and strategy during the Marcomannic Wars on the Danube frontier.

McLynn, Frank. *Marcus Aurelius: Warrior, Philosopher, Emperor*. Da Capo Press, 2009.

> A detailed narrative of Marcus Aurelius as both a military leader and philosopher, with emphasis on his relationship with Commodus and the final campaign against the Germanic tribes in 180 AD.

Harper, Kyle. *The Fate of Rome: Climate, Disease, and the End of an Empire*. Princeton University Press, 2017.

> Discusses the impact of the Antonine Plague on Marcus Aurelius' reign and health, contributing to the context of his death during the campaign on the Danube in 180 AD.

Long, A. A. *Epictetus: A Stoic and Socratic Guide to Life*. Oxford University Press, 2002.

> Examines Stoic philosophy and how Marcus Aurelius applied it to his life, particularly in his approach to death and his legacy.

Sellars, John. *Stoicism*. University of California Press, 2006.

> A modern analysis of Stoicism, useful for understanding the mindset Marcus Aurelius maintained during his rule, especially in the face of death and his concerns about his son, Commodus.

The Battle:

Riley- Smith, Jonathan. *The First Crusade and the Idea of Crusading.* University of Pennsylvania Press, 1986.
>	Provides a detailed account of the First Crusade, including the events leading up to the Battle of Dorylaeum, and explores the motivations and experiences of the Crusaders.

Asbridge, Thomas. *The First Crusade: A New History.* Oxford University Press, 2004.
>	Offers a comprehensive and modern retelling of the First Crusade, including detailed descriptions of the Battle of Dorylaeum and the roles of key figures such as Bohemond of Taranto and Kilij Arslan.

France, John. *Victory in the East: A Military History of the First Crusade.* Cambridge University Press, 1994.
>	Focuses on the military strategies and tactics employed by the Crusaders during the First Crusade, with particular attention to battles like Dorylaeum and the leadership of Bohemond.

Phillips, Jonathan. *The Crusades, 1095–1204.* Routledge, 2014.
>	Explores the broader scope of the Crusades, providing context for the First Crusade and the Battle of Dorylaeum, as well as the significance of the leadership of Bohemond of Taranto.

Norwich, John Julius. *The Normans in the South, 1016- 1130.* Faber & Faber, 1967.
>	Details the rise of the Normans in southern Italy, focusing on Bohemond's lineage and his role in the Crusades, giving insight into his leadership and military background.

Ibn al- Qalanisi. *The Damascus Chronicle of the Crusades: Extracted and Translated from the Chronicle of Ibn al- Qalanisi.* Translated by H.A.R. Gibb, Dover Publications, 2002.
>	A Muslim perspective on the Crusades, offering accounts of the battles and the Crusaders, including leaders like Kilij Arslan, which provides balance to the story.

Runciman, Steven. *A History of the Crusades, Volume I: The First Crusade and the Foundation of the Kingdom of Jerusalem*. Cambridge University Press, 1951.

> A classic work on the Crusades, including the First Crusade and the Battle of Dorylaeum, with detailed descriptions of the people and places involved.

Tyerman, Christopher. *God's War: A New History of the Crusades*. Harvard University Press, 2006.

> Offers a sweeping history of the Crusades, providing context for the religious motivations and military engagements of the Crusaders, including Bohemond's leadership during battles like Dorylaeum.

Setton, Kenneth M. *A History of the Crusades, Volume 1: The First Hundred Years*. University of Wisconsin Press, 1969.

> This multi- volume work provides detailed accounts of the key battles and figures of the Crusades, with particular focus on the First Crusade and the military campaigns led by figures like Bohemond and Kilij Arslan.

Madden, Thomas F. *The Concise History of the Crusades*. Rowman & Littlefield, 2013.

> A succinct overview of the Crusades, covering the essential events of the First Crusade, including the Battle of Dorylaeum, and examining the legacy of the key military and religious leaders involved.